DEATH RA

Bodie burst out from behind the bushes, running like a hound across the concrete. He had eyes for nothing but the canister above Lawson's still motionless shape. Any second now Lawson would hear him ...

Two shots rang out and Lawson's body crumpled. For a moment it had remained upright but now it sank to its knees, the arm still raised, the canister still held high. The pin of the grenade dangled feet above the weapon itself. Four seconds! Bodie knew he had four seconds.

Also by Ken Blake in Sphere Books:

THE PROFESSIONALS 1: WHERE THE JUNGLE ENDS
THE PROFESSIONALS 2: LONG SHOT
THE PROFESSIONALS 3: STAKE OUT
THE PROFESSIONALS 4: HUNTER HUNTED
THE PROFESSIONALS 5: BLIND RUN
THE PROFESSIONALS 6: FALL GIRL
THE PROFESSIONALS 7: HIDING TO NOTHING
THE PROFESSIONALS 8: DEAD RECKONING
THE PROFESSIONALS 9: NO STONE

THE PROFESSIONALS:
Cry Wolf

KEN BLAKE

Based on the original screenplays by
Ranald Graham and Paul Wheeler

SPHERE BOOKS LIMITED
30/32 Gray's Inn Road, London WC1X 8JL

First published by Sphere Books Ltd, 1981

TRADE
MARK

Set in Baskerville

Printed and bound in England by
Cox & Wyman, Reading

Chapter One

The first grey light of dawn touched the crowded fir trees that bordered the eastern limits of the hospital grounds. Everything was silent, even the rooks still and quiet in their branch-top nests. Within minutes the imposing Edwardian building that was Hembury Military Hospital could be clearly seen, its myriad windows shining in the pale sun, the shadow of its gaunt towers cast long across the dew-damp lawns to the west.

Nothing could be heard save the distant hum of a generator, and the occasional, almost inaudible, clatter of dishes from the kitchen where a bleary-eyed staff began the task of making food for the military personnel ensconced within the hospital's grey-brick walls.

A dog ran silently across the sodden turf of the grounds, appearing from the dense woodlands where it had prowled the night away. Anxious, now, to find food, a kennel, a respite from its nocturnal hunting, it was the only movement, the only sign of life; except . . .

Through a window, on the second floor of the west wing, a man who was in agony turned his head to glance at the growing day.

His full name and rank was Lieutenant-Colonel Peter Lawson, and he had begun his final exercise while the night was still deep and pitch black; he stood now, facing the window, a heavy oak chair held above his head. His breathing was becoming laboured. There would be a silence, then a gasping inhalation, and a slight grunt of effort as he maintained this improbable pose.

Eyes narrowed, and filled with sweat, Lawson listened to the monotonous ticking of a clock on the mantelpiece, counting off the seconds, counting the minutes . . .

The blood was high in his cheeks, the muscles of his neck and shoulders tense, taut, almost exploding with the effort of this exercise. But the chair remained high, almost motionless above his head. And his eyes, though filled with pain, blazed with the furious passion of triumph.

And then the smile. The smile that marked the end of his torture, as the sound of the clock registered a time that told him of his success. He could have happily dropped the bulky chair to the floor, but instead he lowered it with arrogant ease, wiping his damp palms across its cushion when it was down, then straightening and rolling his shoulders, massaging his aching arms.

He walked to the window and stared out across the grounds, at the tracks of three dogs in the dew. As he watched, the fourth dog appeared, padding slowly, less eagerly to its kennel, responding to the ultrasonic call of its master.

Peter Lawson grinned as he watched the alsatian vanish. He turned to face the tiny room, its bare walls, bare carpet and tightly made bed a symbol of the white, pure peace that was in his mind.

He was a tall man, wiry and agile, with the deep chest of an athlete, and the hard muscle of a soldier. His hair was blond, and cut short, his face square and thin-lipped, handsome in a cold, almost menacing way. It was hard to look at this man and imagine humour, or love, or respect.

Just ice.

The Iceman.

Now he had to act quickly; but with the practised calm of the military man he was, Lawson did not act with panic. He had not reached the rank of Lieutenant-Colonel through any tendency to spontaneous, terrified action, but through his ability to assess carefully, and to react swiftly, perfectly, and totally.

He opened the two drawers of his wardrobe and selected the clothing he would need. These things he placed in a small leather case. Next he fetched his electric razor and toiletries from the tiny cupboard above his sink. He looked about the room,and picked up the book that lay by his bed: *War in 2080*. After a split-second's hesitation he placed this in the case, and covered these trifling effects with his combat fatigues, which were pressed and clean.

Closing the case, he dried the sweat from his body quickly, then pulled on a smart grey suit; his shirt was high collared, and he wore a tie. He looked every bit the businessman.

But this businessman knew full well that he couldn't leave by the front door.

Lawson raised the window of his room and leaned out to check the ground below. It was a short drop for a man used to the rigours of combat in places as remote as East Africa and Cyprus. The case he dropped flat, and before he jumped from the sill he eased the window down again, landing soon after, and walking briskly, with his idiosyncratic, long-stepping, rather jerky motion across the lawns.

His head held high, his free arm swinging in the military fashion, he was at the woodland in seconds. He trudged through the bracken and undergrowth, and found a thin path that he knew would lead to the outer wall of the area.

Without expression, he attained his goal. If he had been observed at that moment nothing could have been said about him save that in his eyes there was a fixed, single-minded stare . . .

And perhaps, on his lips, just the hint of a smile.

Chapter Two

Lieutenant-Colonel Lawson's escape was discovered exactly half an hour later. In fact, if the car bringing Lawson's friend and superior, Brigadier William Tennant, had not been stopped on the road by an overturned tractor, the Brigadier's visit would have happened before Lawson had quit his room, and the military hospital itself.

Brigadier Tennant was a short, tough soldier, meticulously dressed in his olive green uniform, but without the ostentatious trappings of his rank. He was a man in his mid-fifties, every bit the stereotype of the British commanding officer, from the thin, ginger and grey moustache he wore, to the way he stood with his hands clasped behind his back, peering hard, fixedly at whomever he was addressing.

He waited, now, as Doctor John Lowe came to meet him. Lowe was young, and clearly very tired; his hair was dishevelled, his coat open, his eyes bleary. But he smiled as he greeted the Brigadier, and led the way from the reception area to the stairs and the second floor rooms.

'You've come to see Colonel Lawson, I understand.'

Tennant thought briefly about correcting the mistake in the doctor's reference to rank, but he merely nodded. 'That's right. On my way to Farnsworth. Thought I'd pop by. Knowing Lawson, he'll be awake by now. How is the man?'

Lowe shrugged as he walked, and glanced at the stiff-mannered man beside him. 'Oh, he's well enough.'

It was the wrong thing to say to a tetchy army man. 'Well enough!' Tennant hesitated in his step, then repeated with awesome volume, 'Well enough? In that case, what the blazes is he still doing here?'

Lowe smiled patiently, and opened a swing door for the army man. '*Physically* he's well enough,' he said. 'He's very fit indeed. We've done all the physical and physiological tests that are routine in this sort of case. In fact, we've done them twice. All the lab results are in, if you'd like to inspect them . . . ?'

'Dammit man,' snapped Tennant, 'I've come to see the *boy*, not read through a pile of figures and charts.'

Lowe flushed slightly, but only at the vehemence in this prickly man's demeanour. 'Yes of course. As far as tests are concerned, it's a matter of where do we go from here. I'm beginning to think that only Lawson himself can help us.'

They approached Lawson's room, along a corridor that was white, sterile and distinctly unwelcoming. It smelled strongly of detergent. The doctor, still rankled at Tennant's overbearing attitude, went on, 'Have you by any chance *read* the reports on Colonel Lawson?'

'Glanced at them, old boy. Couldn't understand a blethering word of them. Except the bit about how you don't know what's wrong with Lawson. Understood that all right. God knows what you chaps think you're doing with all that damned equipment.'

'We'll find an answer,' said Lowe softly, and stopped by the door to room 43. He knocked politely, and then repeated the action slightly louder.

'He could still be asleep.'

'Nonsense. Lawson couldn't sleep beyond dawn if he tried.'

Tennant, asserting himself unwelcomely, brushed the young doctor aside and turned the handle of the door. It wouldn't yield and he stood back. Loudly, almost angrily, Tennant said, 'Good God man, you haven't been locking him in, have you? Dammit! He's an officer!'

'It shouldn't *be* locked,' said Lowe, frowning. He too tried the handle. There was a moment's silence, a moment's awful realisation, and then Lowe panicked.

'Nurse! *Nurse!*' He shouted, and began to hammer loudly on the door of the room. 'Colonel Lawson. Can you hear me? Open the door, Colonel.'

A nurse came running along the corridor, white uniform dress riding above her knees, her tiny cap, imperfectly pinned to her hair, flying from her in panic.

'It shouldn't be locked,' she shouted, as she saw the situation. 'And he couldn't have got a key . . . '

She called through the door to Lawson, and again Lowe

tried the handle. This time the door moved slightly.

'It's not locked. It's wedged. Give me a hand.'

Both he and the ageing, irritable Brigadier put their shoulders to the door, slammed hard against the wood and felt it give. Reaching round into the room, Lowe shifted the oak chair from its expertly aligned position below the handle.

The three of them entered the room, for a second startled that it was empty. 'He's gone,' said Lowe unnecessarily, and crossed with Tennant to the window; they stared out at the grounds, at the now dry lawns, where already a handful of nurses and patients were exercising in the early morning. Tennant's gaze rested on the distant, scrubby woodlands, but his focus went beyond, to the countryside and farmlands of this county, and the boundless hiding places available to a man of Lawson's skill and experience.

'Yes,' he said, echoing the doctor's words. 'He's gone. And there's going to be trouble.'

Inasmuch as any member of CI5 could have time off, it had been George Cowley's day off today. He had been relaxing at home, checking through a thick dossier of routine reports, making idle comments in the margins, flipping the pages with ease, almost with disinterest. An excellent Talisker whisky, all of twelve years old, had been his most favoured companion, and a benign feeling of well-being had filled the CI5 chief's senses.

Then the phone had rung, the red phone, the one he would have liked – but hadn't dared – to have taken off the hook.

And of course the call was urgent. Cowley had been at his station for three days, almost non-stop, and they couldn't let him have a moment's peace, a single minute's rest.

Thus it was that by mid-afternoon he found himself strolling in leisurely fashion along a winding country lane, some two miles from the main road to Farnsworth. His own car was pulled off the road a hundred yards ahead, and behind him was the sleek black limousine that had brought Brigadier Tennant to this isolated rendezvous.

Cowley's only consolation was the excellent Havana cigar that Tennant had offered him. He chewed, now, on the last inches of the stubby object, drawing in the sweet, mellow smoke and gazing dreamily into the still distance.

It was an appearance of peace that belied his inner tension. What Tennant had told him had stirred that part of Cowley that had been trained to respond to danger, that could sense impending disaster.

Cowley had known the Brigadier for years. They had been in India together during the war, and their paths had crossed, albeit briefly, during Cowley's stint at MI5. They were not great friends, but Cowley had a great deal of respect for the man, for the fact that Tennant had realised his unsuitability for intelligence work at a time when MI5 was so-called glamorous, and a sure way to achieve the very highest promotion afterwards. Tennant had returned to the army, and settled more comfortably into an organisational role.

He was in civilian clothes now, and wary. His eyes restlessly flickered about the woodland and undergrowth that bordered the lane, and he had already confided to Cowley that he was concerned about Lawson's escape, yesterday, from the hospital at Hembury.

There was a lot more to the story than the Brigadier had let on, and Cowley's almost infallible sense of suspicion had noticed that at once. But he was content enough with what he had heard, sufficient information to convince him that CI5 was needed on the case.

Cowley said, 'I'll tell you what I'll do, Bill. I'll go through that stuff that you've given me, the reports. I'll see if it makes any sense.'

Tennant made a derisive sound. 'Could hardly make head or tail of it myself. Damned language these quacks use . . . enough to make a man cross-eyed. Can't speak plain English. More importantly, have you a man or two available?'

'I'll send a couple of the boys down, to have a look around. They're good lads; if there's anything out of alignment they're likely to sniff it out. They have ways and means at their disposal that I'm a bit long in the tooth to use.'

'Know what you mean, old boy.'

'I'll send them right away.'

Tennant tossed his cigar onto the ground and rubbed it to extinction with his brilliantly polished leather shoe. 'I'd appreciate that.'

They had reached the Brigadier's limousine, and Cowley stopped, staring for a moment at the impassive driver, who was still seated behind the wheel, his *Daily Mirror* now folded respectfully on the seat beside him.

Cowley took Tennant's arm and moved him a few yards away from the car; it was not that he was suspicious of the driver, just that his natural, northern caution allowed not the slightest fraction of a chance to be taken.

'Tell me. Lawson's only close relative is his mother. Am I right in thinking that?'

'Lavinia Lawson. Yes. Wonderful woman.' Tennant's eyes had narrowed and he had turned square on to the CI5 man. 'Why?'

Cowley had intuited the relationship - dead almost certainly - that had existed between Tennant and the escaped man's mother. Rather than soften his questions, he became blunter, the trait for which he was renowned. 'Has she been told anything yet? Anything at all? Have *you*, maybe, said a word or two to her?'

Tennant flushed noticeably, and stiffened slightly. But he shook his head. 'Thinks the boy's still in Germany. I called her last night on some pretext, to try to discover if he'd been in contact ... '

'You gave her no hint ...'

'I know how to guard my tongue, George. Surprised at you.'

'Of course.'

Tennant hesitated, then looked sharply at the other man. 'I should ask one thing of you ... '

Cowley smiled amiably. 'What's that, Bill?'

'If there's any nasty news ... Any bad news ... You know what I mean. If there's anything like that, I should like to be the one to tell her.'

Cowley bowed his head slightly in an affirmation. 'Of course.'

As they returned to the car, Tennant thrust his hands deep into his great-coat pockets, and his head lowered slightly. 'I was with her husband – Lawson's father – I was there when he was killed in Malaya . . . Had to break that one to her as well . . . Brought us a little closer. No need to go into details. A great family, the Lawsons. All given their lives for their country. Generations of them . . . Have great respect for the Lawsons, even young Peter. Sad business . . . '

Cowley experienced a moment's discomfort as Tennant's sentimentality threatened to linger; but the soldier was aware of his own weakness and he snapped out of the maudlin mood, straightened and extended his hand to Cowley. 'Well, must be off. Sorry to have dragged you away from your whisky. Must have lunch soon. My treat.'

'Goodbye Bill. I'll remember that.'

The projection room was small, cramped and hot. Cowley sat in the back row of seats, his arm stretched out, his legs crossed. In front of him, Ray Doyle and Bodie were two dishevelled shapes, their tired faces eerily lit by reflected light from the screen.

As Cowley spoke, so the light flickered as new slides appeared, reflected in the CI5 men's eyes as they intently studied the subject before them.

It was very early morning; very early indeed. After losing his twenty-four hours rest yesterday, Cowley had been in no mood to stand on ceremony and allow his two lads the luxury of even an extra minute's lie in. They had been called at five. Sharp. And their objections had been overruled.

Sharply.

The call had been disastrous for Bodie. He hadn't yet been to bed, but after a long, stealthy, tactical night's talking, he had sensed himself on the verge of success: her name had been Jan Huxley, and she was the tallest girl that Bodie had ever fallen in lust with. But she had been unwilling to succumb to his charms; at least, she had been unwilling to succumb too quickly.

It was a wearying, and often frustrating business, trying to tempt the opposite sex to sample the youthful wares of an athlete. When the call from HQ had come, abruptly shattering the mood of exquisite sexual tension, Jan had laughed, straightened her long, thigh-split skirt about her shapely frame, and walked from the apartment, leaving Bodie to swear as loudly and as vehemently as posible down the phone –

At George Cowley. Who was not amused.

Bodie sat, now, his smooth, sullen face pale in the white light, his lips turned down at the edge, his mind still half on the girl as he absorbed the information about Lieutenant-Colonel Peter Lawson.

Ray Doyle had been less disturbed by the early call. In fact, Ray Doyle was highly amused at Bodie's disgruntlement. His tousled hair even more in disarray (he had not had time to drag a comb through his unruly mop before racing for his car), he fidgeted in his seat, trying to get comfortable, but slowly became more serious, more intent, as the facts about Lawson grew in his mind. And as Cowley's deep concern began to impinge upon his unconsciousness.

The stills were a succession of photographs of Colonel Lawson, his known associates, the hospital, his barracks, his records and his favoured weaponry. The morning had begun with a typical Cowley blunt statement, into which the two CI5 operatives were expected to read a volume of information:

'Lieutenant-Colonel Peter Lawson. Royal Tank Regiment. Disappeared. Two days ago.'

Now, as the slide sequence finished, the aspects of the event could be discussed.

Bodie was slightly puzzled. 'I don't get it,' he said, staring hard at the cold, ruthless image of Lawson that watched him from the screen. 'He was in a Military Hospital, right?'

'Correct,' said Cowley from behind. 'In the heart of the Hampshire countryside.'

'And he walked out. Just like that. Nobody saw him, nobody made any attempt to stop him.'

Cowley's voice was soft, accented, patient. 'We don't know that he *walked* out.'

'But he wasn't locked up, right?' put in Ray Doyle. 'I mean, it wasn't the sort of place with bars three millimetres apart, and forty locks with forty keys.'

'No locks. Freedom of movement,' said Cowley. 'But a lot of security. It's a military hospital after all.'

Bodie shook his head. 'Could he have discharged himself?

Taken responsibility etcetera? Just decided that he was better, and gone?'

'It's a slim possibility, but only slim. And there's a solid piece of evidence against him having discharged himself.'

'That evidence being ... ?' said Doyle restlessly, still regarding the face of Lawson.

'If he had discharged himself,' said Cowley, leaning forward to rest his arms on the back of Doyle's chair, 'He would presumably have returned to his regiment.'

Bodie nodded understanding. 'Which he hasn't.'

'Quick aren't you,' said Doyle mischievously.

Bodie ignored him sourly. 'So when did he vanish, did you say?'

'Two days ago. Sometime before dawn.'

Doyle smirked as he said, 'Then he's absent without leave. What a naughty boy.'

Cowley ignored the latter comment, and said, 'Technically, yes. Lawson is AWOL. He was, as it were, *posted* to the hospital where he was undergoing a series of check-ups.'

Together, Doyle and Bodie said, 'What sort of check-ups?' And they grinned, facing each other, as they were caught in the echo of each other's eagerness.

Cowley's gaze rested thoughtfully upon the image of Lawson for a moment. Then he sat back in his chair and said, grimly, 'Something happened in Europe. Something bad. It was during a recent military exercise, which was taking place under Lawson's command. Almost certainly in Western Germany, and probably close to the border, the army isn't telling exactly what happened and where, which makes me think that it was "observed". They're in a panic about it, still, and it happened some months ago.'

Bodie said quietly, 'And Lawson was the culprit ...'

'Culprit or victim, it's hard to tell. The army didn't know, and the army protects its own ...'

'As long as they're officers,' said Doyle with just a hint of sarcasm in his voice. He had folded his arms, wide dark eyes filled with the stoney glare of the escaped soldier.

Cowley ignored Doyle's petulance. 'Whatever it was that Lawson got up to, or caused to go wrong, his Command HQ decided it was hospital he needed, and not the brig. They flew him home, to Hembury, and began to put him through the most exhaustive phsyical and psychiatric tests.'

Doyle turned slightly as he asked, 'Do we know the results of those tests? Or is that covered?'

'No, it's not secret,' said Cowley, a note of resignation in his voice. 'Physically the man was fit as . . . well, as fit as you two. And he's years older. Mentally, the results, I gather, are inconclusive. The full barrage of psychiatric tests had not finished, however, before Lieutenant-Colonel Lawson packed his suitcase and made good his french leave.'

Doyle grinned and straightened up, warming to the idea of the role he and Bodie were to play. 'And all you want us to do is to comb through the Home Counties and find him.'

'Find him, or find out what has happened to him. It's not just a find the looney task. Not necessarily.'

Bodie and Doyle exchanged uneasy glances. Something in Cowley's voice had pricked their suspicious natures.

'Find out what happened to him,' repeated Bodie. 'And just what might that be?'

Cowley folded his hands across the backs of his two agent's chairs, leaning between them as he said, more softly, 'Lawson's regiment plays a vital role in NATO's first line of defence against land attack from Warsaw Pact countries. I don't know exactly where he was stationed, but I do know that Lawson himself has a crucial role in those battle plans. He had access at the highest level to military secrets in that particular theatre . . . '

'And a little planned madness,' said Doyle with the faintest of nods, 'To make it easier for him to be kidnapped.'

'To defect,' said Bodie solemly. 'It's too obvious . . . '

'Nevertheless,' said Cowley from behind, 'It's a possibility that has to be borne in mind. If Lawson *has* been kidnapped, or if he has defected, then many of those plans will have to be changed, and that could involve the War Office in months of work.'

'And the enemy will be aware of that,' said Doyle. Grimly.

Bodie said, 'Striking while the iron is soft. But if the Russians *had* grabbed him, then he would've been in Moscow within twenty-four hours . . . '

'Right,' said Doyle loudly, 'And we'd have heard about it

pretty soon from MI5. Within hours. Our contacts are good there.'

'But we haven't heard,' said Bodie.

Doyle shook his tousle-haired head, and the hint of a smile touched his full lips. 'Otherwise we wouldn't be sitting here now.'

'Until we hear or learn otherwise,' murmured Cowley, 'We must assume that Lawson is still in this country, and that others are equally as eager as ourselves to learn his whereabouts, or possibly his state of mind.'

'In other words,' came Bodie's quiet voice, 'We want to find him before Ivan the Terrible . . . '

'Correct,' said Cowley. 'And remember, this is a low key, low profile operation. He is not listed as a missing person, and he will not be reported absent without leave. We want to keep it in the family for as long as possible. As long as we can. Without compromising ourselves.'

Ray Doyle rubbed his jaw, uncomfortable in the hot, cramped room, eager to get out into the fresh air again. 'Let's have another look at that first shot, the recent mug shot.'

There was a moment's flickering of light, and then the tall, athletic figure of Lawson appeared on the screen; he was wearing his fatigues, holding a small calibre weapon, and staring at the camera with a stern, angry expression.

Doyle wondered, idly, what had happened to the photographer immediately afterwards.

Bodie grinned cynically, 'Not exactly a barrel of laughs, is he?'

Ray Doyle smiled, then thought of something and frowned slightly. 'If he's got amnesia, then maybe he's forgotten all his military secrets as well. It's a possibility, isn't it?'

'Tell you what,' said Bodie impassively.

'What?'

'He doesn't look the forgetful type.'

The briefing session over, there was only the personal file to be gone through, and that was the sort of study that Bodie and Doyle liked to do 'on the wheel'.

After a frustratingly slow passage out of London, they

were at last onto the M3 motorway, and the sleek Capri hummed past other cars on the freeway under the expert, gentle touch of Bodie. Bodie liked to drive, and often squabbled with his team-mate over who should sit behind the wheel. These days they tended to apply Cowley's own instructions, delivered as to who, among them, should take the upper hand in any situation: first one there takes the initiative. No argument.

Bodie had fairly sprinted across the Home Office parking lot, and gone into the Capri through the window, an ostentatious, and slightly painful entry, that had reduced Ray Doyle to laughter.

Bodie was still tired from his sleepless, luckless night. Ray Doyle had been drinking with an ex-policeman friend of his the night before, remembering the good old days in the Metropolitan, and reflecting rather miserably upon the way attitudes to the police had changed in the last few years.

It had been fun to be a copper then; now, he'd not go back for all the gold in Johannesburg.

He was flipping through the folder – a buff coloured container, marked grandly 'Limited Availability' – looking for the snippets of information on Peter Lawson that would help them build a mental profile of the man, and perhaps glean some clue as to his likely actions after the event of his escape.

It was all terribly familiar to Doyle. Lawson was a typical army officer, with a typical army officer's background.

As Bodie streaked the car southwards, eyes ever wary for a parked patrol car (they hated to get held up when on a mission) Doyle read out what he was finding.

'Eton.'

'Of course,' said Bodie.

'There *was* a chance he might have gone to Birkenhead.'

'No chance at all. How'd he fare on the great playing fields?'

'Colours in cricket,' read Doyle, 'Rowing, and rugby. No athletics, though ... Oh, wait a minute ... ' He turned pages.

Bodie said, 'I thought they didn't play eton at Rugby.'

'Come again?' Doyle looked up, glanced past his partner at the flashing landscape of Surrey, glanced at the clock and saw the needle touching a hundred.

'Skip it,' said Bodie, not prepared to elaborate on his silly humour. It was still far too early.

Doyle grimaced as the feeble joke finally got through to him. He bent back to the task of reading, his blue eyes flashing down the lines of type, expertly assessing the information.

'Here it is. Christ, this boy's a real challenge. Sandhurst training after school. Sword of Honour. And Pentathlon Captain.'

Bodie glanced away from the road at the folder, his solemn, pugnacious face hardly changing expression to manifest his comment that, '*Now* I'm impressed.'

'Thought you would be. Olympic contender in the late sixties, but forced to withdraw because of army duties . . . '

'Must have been special duties,' said Bodie, steering the car along the inside of a juggernaut that was hogging the outer lane. 'Army revels in Olympic medals.'

Doyle went on, 'Rackets. Rowing. Cricket.'

'At least they taught him the three "R's".'

'Then he was commissioned to the 60th rifles . . . four years later he was transferred over to the SAS . . . '

'Hard man, eh?'

'Four years with the SAS. Captain Staff College . . . G.2 Ops . . . made Major there . . . Then BAOR . . . Lieutenant-Colonel at age 37! Battalion Commander . . . His own regiment . . . Europe . . . '

'Crack up.'

'Too much pressure. Too much responsibility. Too young.'

'But still, not what you'd call an outsider in the promotion stakes.'

Doyle agreed. 'Groomed for the top.'

'A strong case of what you might call upward mobility. Power assisted.'

'He's gone through those ranks like food through a goose.'

Bodie scowled. 'That's downward.'

'Horizontal.'

'Fast, anyway,' said Bodie. A black sports car overtook him and he whistled as he checked his own speedometer. 'Bloody royals.' Glancing at Doyle, and then looking pointedly at the folder, he said, 'Well come on then. Leave the sparkling career – let's get down to the juicy bits.'

'You mean the psychiatric reports.'

'Yeah. The dirt.'

With an ex-policeman's precision, Ray Doyle sorted through the pages until he came to the thick sheaf of pink carbon copies on which the results of Lawson's examination by a psychiatric team were recorded; preceding those tests was the extensive army folio that had been compiled during Lawson's career in the military. It was to this detailed profile of one of Britain's top officers that Doyle addressed his attention, and was soon feeling baffled.

'Which would you like first? Psychomorphological, or psychopathological?'

Bodie gave Doyle one of his typical, withering stares, then shook his head in disgust.

'Isn't there anything under girlfriends?'

Chapter Three

Once, he had been hunted across the African veldt; an unarmed, wounded man, pursued by the cream of the S.W.I.F.A. guerrillas that had driven his 'adopted' nation out of power in the country.

He had not been found.

There had been no cover on the veldt; it had been cold by night, cold enough to freeze the marrow in his bones, and it had been hot during the day, hot enough to boil his brains.

The blacks who had hunted him were trained fighters, trained trackers, mercenaries like himself, gaining experience in the field before moving on to assume positions of command in the respectable, official armies of their countries.

But they had not found him.

Years later, Lawson negotiated the English countryside with almost contemptuous ease. He knew just how to make himself invisible, even to dogs. He knew exactly how to use cover, the cover of trees, of bushes, of flat ground.

Unless he wished it, nobody would find him. And for the moment at least, he didn't wish to be found.

He was carrying his suitcase still, and he had not changed his clothes for two days. He was muddied, and he was weary. He looked like a tramp. This was part of the effectiveness, for people rarely stop to pay attention to a vagabond.

The one thing that had not changed in his two days of walking was the fiercely determined look in his eyes. He was tired, of that there could be no doubt; his eyes were rimmed with fatigue, and his skin had that pallid, drawn appearance that is associated with lack of sleep.

But Peter Lawson knew exactly where he was going, and exactly how long he had to get there. And until he arrived, he would not rest, would not stop.

He was almost at his destination now. He walked across

fields, and through woodland with a stiff backed, regular stride, his case held beside him, his free arm swinging. He walked along the quieter roads, but ducked into cover each time he heard the approach of a car. He sheltered occasionally in barns, or out-houses, and had fed well on apples, eggs, and the scraps of food that are always to be found in the area of a farm habitation.

In these last hours of his solitary journey, he checked his bearings, using a detailed Ordnance-Survey map (much covered with his own coded notations) and a small, exquisitely made compass. He checked the sun, the alignment of the land, the flight of birds.

Lawson knew how to read everything, even the shadows on the grass.

So precisely did he know his direction that even a road was just one more unnatural feature to be traversed between one wooded ditch and the next field of immature corn. He used the land as a motorist uses the Highway Code. He was a man at home with nature, hiding within it, using its natural features to make his passage to the west easier, and safer.

And thus, with the confidence and silence of a hunter, the tall, cold man came within first sight of the tiny, rural town of Cornbrook.

For an instant he hesitated, unsure for the first time, for the town was bigger than he had expected.

But then he picked up his case again and began to cross a fallow field, skirting the small graveyard of the local, ramshackle Saxon church, and arriving in the span of two or three minutes at the beginning of the town's main street. There were a few cars parked there, and a handful of shoppers, but the town was the centre of a vast farming society, and only on market days did Cornbrook bustle with life.

He walked along the pavement, feeling certain pangs: of hunger, of a need for strong, black coffee; of a need for the company of a woman, the simple, animal instinct that he could suppress so easily.

He was more aware here of the filth on his pressed, pinstriped suit, of the strange contrast between his natural bearing, and the dishevelled tone of his immediate appearance. But he met no one's gaze, and he aroused only a passing interest. He walked stiffly, and swiftly along the short high street, and turned into a side road on the far side of the town.

Here, a small, yellow façaded cafe welcomed him to the end of his journey.

If Len Clarke had ever entertained ideas of a better life, he had entertained them more than ten years before, in the days when he had been a fitter man, and a better man, and had enjoyed the company of men in the 60th rifles.

He had left the army to get married, and to set up on his own in a business that he had always reckoned he would enjoy. But his wife had run off with a commercial traveller, and the business had got steadily worse each year since that fateful Autumn when the new dual carriageway had opened to the west, and lorries just never came through Cornbrook any more.

A few of the smaller haulage contractors still knew where to get the best egg and chips west of Basingstoke, and took the short detour through the sleepy village, parking on the outskirts of the place, and walking to the warm, if unkempt, cafe where their old mate 'Nobby' would be only too pleased to see them. Trade, though, was never brisk, even if the food was good. Nobby could not afford more than one waitress, and he did most of the cooking and serving himself.

On the particular afternoon that his old regimental Colonel came to visit, the cafe was more than half full, and Nobby Clarke was working half again as hard as usual. There were several truckers in a group, noisily discussing football and hitch-hikers they had picked up and won favours from. The tea was being drunk like beer, and the cafe was hot and steamy.

Nobby himself was not in a sociable mood. He was a small, hard-looking man, his fair hair receding fast from his head, his eyes small and grey and pig-like. His forearms were covered with tattooes and he still had that muscley, no-nonsense look about him that had helped him with the middle-weight boxing championships of his old army regiment.

He looked up at the tall, solemn man who suddenly stepped into the cafe from the street and let his case fall to the ground as he stood there. He looked again, hesitating in the act of pouring tea into a cup.

Something about the stranger . . .

The man in the doorway stared at him, and then raised his right hand in the briefest, most cynical of salutes.

And Nobby Clarke recognised Peter Lawson, and his heart near leapt into his throat.

'My God, it's the Colonel,' he said quietly, placing the tea-pot down on the counter, wiping his hands on his flowery apron, and stepping out from behind the serving area.

He approached Lawson in near disbelief.

'Colonel Lawson . . . It is you, isn't it sir?'

Lawson stood quite still, gazing piercingly at Nobby, as if sizing him up, or trying to remember something about him.

But Lawson knew the small man all right. It was Nobby he had come to find, come across tens of miles of rolling, difficult country, without sleep, and with only snatched meals.

The years had aged the little man more than Lawson would have expected. Boredom, perhaps, had marked itself in the slight listlessness of the soldier; too much tea and chips had swollen his belly, and puffed up his cheeks. But Lawson could see the streak of hardness there, he could re-envision the tough, wiry, tenacious little soldier that Len Clarke had been years before.

'What are you doing here, sir?' Clarke asked, frowning as he stared at the impassive Lawson. He was a little like a dog, Lawson thought. Ready to go for the throat of the enemy at the slightest hint of danger, but meek, and gentle and able to be dominated by its master.

Lawson felt his thoughts slip away from the plan, from the driving, burning plan that had carried him this far; he needed Clarke for that plan, for the incredible mission that he was about to commence. But he needed, first, to remember just how good the tough little northerner had been . . . And could be again. Lawson let his mind become a tape recorder, playing back the scenes in West and South East Africa, scenes of violence, of danger, of impossible achievement, achieved with real panache. Clarke carrying two men through the bush, while Lawson protected the rear of the tiny troop mission, the two of them the sole survivors of a perilous journey through guerrilla infested territory, and alone hitting the wood and mud hut that was the local HQ . . . Taking it out . . . Wiping it out . . .

Slinking back into the undergrowth, and retracing their steps to safety.

It was memories of the little man's tenacity that relaxed the cord of tension in Lawson's tight sprung body. His gaze came back to the chubby man before him, and the flesh seemed to fall away from Len Clarke, the muscles tighten, the gleam in his eyes take on that edge of mischief that Lawson had valued.

'Nobby,' he said, 'I need a couple of good men.'

Nobby Clarke reflected back Lawson's intensely grave stare. For a moment both men were silent, but Lawson's silence was that of a man waiting, whereas Nobby's moment of quiet was accompanied by a sudden excitement, burning in his eyes.

A mission!

Lawson could almost hear the cogs and the clockwork whirring.

He's come to get me for a *mission.* I'm going to fight again! With the Colonel. The Colonel and me, and maybe two or three others . . .

Action!

Nobby said, relaxing slightly. 'You've found one, of course. You know that sir.'

'Do I, Nobby?'

The doubt in the small man's face was quite conspicuous. He'd spent years building up this shoddy little cafe. It was all he had. He was beginning to be torn, torn between security . . . And love.

Nobby Clarke balked at the idea of having to commit himself fully. But Lawson had time, plenty of time . . . Almost a full week of time. He had planned everything down to the last detail, and recruitment and re-enlistment were two factors that he was sure he had not underestimated.

Men did not return to the field of war after ten years away without a certain coaxing.

Nobby said, 'Come and sit down, Colonel. You may need a couple of good men, but right now you look more like you need a good meal.'

'I've eaten sufficiently for the body, Nobby. But thanks.'

'A Len Clarke special never does you harm. Eggs, bacon, chips and a steak on the side that'll melt in your mouth.'

They sat at a corner table, away from the noisy gang of truckers, and out of earshot of the two other patrons of the grease joint, a sullen faced woman, and a hitch-hiker. Nobby called over the waitress and placed Lawson's order for him. Lawson didn't even glance at the buxom young blonde, her body exaggeratedly full in the tight mini-skirt and revealing blouse. She glanced at the Colonel and frowned as he ignored her. Then she turned back to the counter and began to prepare the food.

'Two men,' said Lawson, staring hard at the other. He scratched at his stubble as he spoke. 'Two good men.'

'And what would these two good men be used for?'

Lawson hesitated before he answered, but his eyes never left Nobby's. At length he said, 'A mission.'

'What kind of mission? Like in the old days? Abroad?' Nobby felt excitement rise in his breast. But Lawson was giving very little away. He shook his head.

'Not abroad, Nobby. Not this time.'

'What sort of mission, then?'

Lawson leaned forward, hands folded before him. Nobby responded by leaning forward too, so that their faces were almost touching, and Lawson's stale breath was sharp and unpleasant.

'Top secret, Nobby. Can't tell you yet.'

Nobby Clarke sat back, slightly uncomfortable. Suddenly he was uneasy, he didn't like the sound of that 'top secret'. He glanced down at Lawson's muddy suitcase, and at the mud and leaf litter that still coated the bottoms of the Colonel's fancy trousers. He looked at the unshaven, dishevelled man. For a moment not even Lawson's steely gaze, that ultra-confidence that radiated from his hard eyes, could banish the old soldier's doubts.

'Is this official?'

'Undercover,' said Lawson.

There was a moment's further silence, save for the clatter

of cutlery on plates, and the noise of the raucous driving group; Nobby Clarke tried desperately to digest this input, to make some sense of it with his limited mental resources.

'Undercover, eh? We've been undercover a few times, ain't we, Colonel? Africa, under that sodding dripping jungle . . . Out in Germany, in those forests.'

'I remember the forests, Nobby. Dry during the rain, sheltering beneath the trees, and then sopping wet for hours as the rain filtered through.'

Nobby grinned at the reminiscence. 'Real undercover work that was. But this . . . This top secret stuff. I mean, it's spy stuff, is it? Plain clothes . . . all that?'

'A special uniform, Nobby.'

'Be good to get back into uniform. I'd like that, Colonel, I'd like that a lot. Been a long time, the old uniform, tucked away, packed away. I'd like to wear that again.'

'You kept your clothes, did you?' Lawson's eyes had narrowed for the first time, and he seemed thoughtful.

Nobby grinned. 'You know me, Colonel. Never could leave anything in place unless it was chained down. Got quite a haul out back, quite a little haul. The barracks won't notice. I don't suppose they noticed anything was missing, even the bed.'

He chuckled as he thought of the single bed, up in the spare room, that he had only lifted for a joke, and had got away with so well that he'd not seen the point of taking it back.

'And weapons . . . ?' prompted Lawson. He leaned forward again. Nobby Clarke touched one nail-bitten forefinger to the side of his nose and winked. 'As I said, Colonel. Never could resist collecting a souvenir or three. Got quite a little armoury.'

'I'd like to see . . .'

Nobby leaned towards Lawson, glancing at the waitress, who was chatting to one of the truckers across the counter. He called out to her, 'Hey, Doreen, where's that food?'

'Steak's not done yet,' she called back, sullenly and with the loudest hint of a pout; and turned back to the engaging young man who was chatting her up.

Lawson said, again, 'I'd like to see those pieces, Nobby. You wouldn't mind that, would you?'

'I'm not so sure, Colonel.' He was uncomfortable again. He thought - though he couldn't be sure - that Lawson was trying to put one over on him. It was Lawson's appearance. Lawson had always been so smart, so precise, even in the bush. It wasn't right for the man to look so seedy.

He said, as Lawson watched him quietly, 'This mission . . . it is army, isn't it? I mean, it is *official*.'

Lawson shook his head slowly. 'Higher than Army. Much higher. High as you can get. Army . . . They're just pawns, small fry.'

'Higher than the Army. Mother o' God. Higher than the Army. What could that be, Colonel?' Lawson's eyes bored into him, and Nobby felt dizzy with the effort of thinking . . . It had just been too long, too long away. His mind was fuddled, no longer on edge, ready to respond. He had learned to ask too many questions. That was it. Too many questions. Needed to get back to that simple, effective obedience.

And yet . . .

He wanted to know!

'Higher . . . you mean like Secret Service?'

'Higher than that, even,' said Lawson, and smirked just slightly as Nobby repeated the word and shook his head.

'The Queen . . . It must have something to do with the Queen,' he said, and Lawson actually laughed, reached out and grabbed Nobby's hand, squeezing the flesh until the bones threatened to spark against each other. Solemnly, the Colonel said, 'Keep your voice down, Nobby.'

'I understand, sir.'

Lawson looked quickly around the cafe. Nobody was taking any notice of them. 'Something else, Nobby. Something important. There's a great deal - a *very* great deal - of money involved in this mission. Money like you never dreamed of. Enough money to buy the Ritz. Think about that.'

Nobby was thinking all right. His mind, from its befuddled state had suddenly become clear, throbbing with expectation.

'What would we have to do?' He noticed that Doreen was wiping her hand across her nose, a sure sign that she was about to dish up Lawson's plate of food.

The Colonel gripped Nobby's wrist, eyes ablaze. 'You have to show courage! Loyalty! Determination!'

Nobby licked his lips, visions of money dancing in his head.

'Are you *with* me, man!' said Lawson fiercely, his voice rising slightly.

'Maybe ...' said Nobby hesitantly, then, caught in the blazing conviction from Lawson's face, he said more determinedly, 'We'll talk some more when you've eaten. This could be the start of something!'

'Good man, Sergeant! Good man!'

With a satisfying squeal of brakes, Bodie ran the Capri off the narrow country road and to a stop on the bumpy grass verge at its side. Doyle put out a hand to the glove compartment, to steady himself as Bodie finished his James Hunt routine, grinning briefly as he sat back in the driver's seat.

'Not a bad time from London,' he said.

'Shame about my breakfast,' retorted Doyle, and grinned boyishly. He unclipped his belt and turned to stare at the high, red brick wall beside them. 'Let's go.'

The two CI5 men left the car and ran smartly up to the wall. Doyle turned his back against it, clasped his hands together, and braced himself as Bodie - quickly, and sure-footedly - used this hand-made sling to leap to the very top of the high barrier.

'No glass, no wire,' he called down, peering over into the dense undergrowth, and pine-woodland beyond.

'What about the drop?' gasped Doyle from below, trying to get his mop of fair hair out of Bodie's knee-range.

'Long. An army man, though ... Well, a cinch. Olympic standard. Wouldn't catch your country bobby making it without a trampoline ...'

'But Lawson could've?'

'If he's the athlete he's cracked up to be, yeah.'

A car drove past and Doyle tried to look innocent, smiling and nodding at the puzzled passengers. 'Up we go,' he called, then, and gave Bodie an extra shove. Bodie lay supine along the top of the ivy and moss-covered wall, and pulled his team mate up and over, dropping to the ground himself with a crouch, and a spring.

Then, running with their practised stoop, keeping low behind the cover, they split from each other and began to weave towards the hospital lawns. Within seconds neither could see the other.

'Once in here,' called Doyle, his voice already muffled to Bodie's sharp ears, 'Not even the dogs could have got him.'

Bodie agreed silently, darting from tree to bush, worming his way through an open patch of grass, and swiftly coming within eyeshot of the dull grey building ahead.

At the edge of the cover, facing the lawns, where nurses and patients strolled in leisurely fashion, Doyle and Bodie checked each other out, and grinned.

'Transit time, if he was shifting, no more than thirty seconds.'

'Agreed,' said Doyle. 'The lawn?'

Bodie assessed the distance across the open ground to the base of the tall, west wing wall, from which Lawson had perhaps jumped, and to the small, front exit, from which the Colonel had possibly made good his escape.

'Forty seconds to the wall. Fifty to the exit.'

'Go,' called Doyle. 'And watch out for wheelchairs.'

'Enjoying himself hugely, Bodie began to sprint. He weaved expertly through the startled population of the grounds, hardly breathing as he pounded across the grass, legs pumping, face grim with effort.

He flung himself against the wall, turned and watched as Doyle trotted casually after him.

'Good run,' called Doyle. 'Thirty eight seconds.'

Bodie was hardly touched with perspiration, though his heart was hitting him quite hard.

They walked to the exit, acknowledging the still-startled nurses with a pleasant wave, and trotted up the steps and into the foyer.

'Lawson could have been out of the grounds in four minutes,' they agreed. 'Less if he was truly fit, though at nearly forty years old that would still be large percentages slower than us.'

Doctor John Lowe fetched them up to the vacant room, then, and for the first time the two agents could assess the extent of the possible jump from the window.

'Are you sure he went out here?' asked Ray Doyle, pulling the window up and leaning out. It was a long way down. Even he would have had to compose himself for the drop.

Doctor Lowe shrugged, reached out and pulled round the heavy oak chair in the room. 'He'd wedged this under the door handle. Unless he managed to do that from outside, it's hard to see how else he could have got away.'

'Easiest thing in the world,' said Bodie quietly, and when Lowe glanced at him, he stabbed a finger at the chair. 'Wedging that on the inside from the outside. Classic locked room mystery.'

'Fancies himself as Sherlock Bodie,' said Doyle with a cheeky grin as he tried fitting the chair under the handle and found that it worked extremely well. It took quite a jolt to budge the door enough to tell that it wasn't actually locked. Doyle replaced the chair in the room, looked around, wrinkled up his nose.

It was a bare, sterile place, without personality, without warmth. Lawson had made no effort at all to shape these tiny quarters into a relaxing den, during his stay here. He had quite obviously been determined to make that stay as short as possible.

'No one saw him *outside*?' he asked after a moment.

'No,' said Doctor Lowe. 'The kitchen staff would have been hard at it, the generator room was starting up, and the caretaker would have been down there. He went very early in the morning, that's clear enough.'

'How about dogs?' asked Bodie, impassively watching the young doctor.

'Four dogs in the grounds, but they get called in after dawn. He must have known that, I suppose . . .'

'I suppose,' echoed Bodie.

Ray Doyle was at the window, hands thrust into the pockets of his tight jeans, shoulders hunched thoughtfully. 'How many exits from the grounds?'

Lowe said, 'There's the main gate. But he could have got out anywhere. Climbed over the wall where it's low. Some parts don't even have walls.'

'In other words,' said Doyle, turning from the window

and regarding the other man with a cold, almost patronising expression, 'The security in this place is the next best thing to rotten.'

Lowe flushed bright red. He didn't like the arrogance of this pair of young agents at all, their brash, super cool attitude, their radiant sense of superiority. 'It *is* a hospital,' he said. 'It's not a prison.'

'How convenient. The Russians *never* take military personnel from a red cross area, of course.'

Bodie stepped in at this moment, thinking that Lowe might suddenly cease to be very co-operative with them. 'Doctor. We've looked over the psychiatric reports in some detail . . .'

He noticed Doyle's reaction out of the corner of his eyes. He went on. 'My colleague here found them a little hard going, isn't that right, Ray?' He smiled sweetly at Doyle, who folded his arms, shook his head and leaned back against the sill of the window. 'We were wondering if you could give us something more concise to, er, to get our teeth into . . . ?'

Lowe frowned for a second, 'Well . . .'

'Preferably in a nutshell!' finished Bodie.

'What I can tell you,' said the doctor carefully, 'Is that Colonel Lawson was posted here for examination, because apparently he had suffered some sort of nervous breakdown during military manoeuvres. How precisely that breakdown manifested itself is not something that we were told. I'm afraid.'

Doyle was astonished. 'You weren't *told*?'

'I'm afraid not.'

Bodie exchanged a glance with his colleague. There was definitely something very strange going on here. 'But didn't you find out? You were Lawson's psychiatrist . . .'

Lowe shrugged. 'We would have presumably learned something of the nature of his breakdown, but we didn't get round to it.'

'Why not?' persisted Bodie.

Lowe bristled. 'We were investigating his present personality rather than his previous actions.'

'Well, how *was* he?' asked Ray Doyle.

'When he first arrived, he was clearly disturbed. To the expert eye, at least.'

'Disturbed in what way?' prompted Bodie. The word itself meant little to him, in fact, came close to that area of incomprehensible jargon that he associated with medicine these days.

'Nothing at all obvious,' reflected Lowe. 'In fact, quite the opposite. He was just *too* calm, too relaxed.'

Bodie wasn't sure that anyone could ever be too calm; it sounded like a useful trait in a man who would have to make life and death decisions. External calmness did not necessarily mean that the adrenalin wasn't flowing, sharpening and quickening the mind. He himself, as part of his training for his stint in Ulster, during the troubles, had been taught how to mask the churning, gut-fear inside him. Keep calm, but let the blood heat slightly, to keep you on your toes.

'Did he co-operate?' he asked. 'Or was it dumb silence?'

Lowe shook his head. 'No, no. He co-operated quite actively, quite willingly. He had too, of course. It was his duty. His career was at stake.'

Ray Doyle was getting fidgety. He and Bodie had been told so little: just, find out what happened to Lawson. He wasn't yet clear just exactly what the problem was. He and Bodie often were forced to operate in a vacuum, but this vacuum was a little too cold.

'Look,' he said, trying to keep the irritation in his voice to a minimum. 'This isn't going to go beyond us. Leave aside the technicalities and just tell us how did *you* actually find him. What were *your* impressions?'

'Your gut impressions,' said Bodie.

Lowe took a deep breath and ran his well-manicured hand through his thinning hair. 'From the little I *did* see of him, my guess is that he'd had some kind of profound shock. Now, that shock may either have been shock *at* his own actions - whatever they were - or the cause of those actions. In either case, it seemed to me that he was fighting a battle inside himself - a desperate battle - to maintain his own clarity . . .'

'I've seen that myself,' said Bodie. 'After Korea . . . And in the years before the heavy duty in Nam.'

'It's a familiar syndrome in military men in one way,' agreed Lowe. 'And if you're thinking of the sort of shock to the system that brainwashing involves, then yes, there were similarities. But this man, this Lawson, I'd have said no to any sort of unconscious programming. Unless there's been a substantial advance in techniques, out east . . .'

Bodie said. 'So if he ran off, if he was acting on his own initiative, how do you interpret that action?'

Lowe shrugged again, and walked to stare out of the window. 'It might be as simple as a deep-seated urge to get away. He may have felt that he could work it all out on his own, and work it out better.'

'Sounds reasonable to me,' said Doyle gruffly. He narrowed his eyes, questioningly, at Bodie, who shrugged slightly and agreed.

Lowe turned from the window. 'I agree with you. Quite reasonable. But he *should* have told us. He had to request it.'

'If he had requested leave,' said Bodie, 'Would you have granted it, bearing in mind his condition?'

Lowe went on the defensive, 'I couldn't have granted anything. Only a superior officer . . . My rank's Major . . .'

'Never mind the rank,' said Bodie, piercingly, almost with hostility. 'As a doctor, what would your recommendation have been?'

'I'd have refused permission. Definitely.'

'You mean, he's not well enough to have been let out.'

Lowe turned to Doyle, hesitated, then nodded. 'He may still be trying to help himself in his own best way.'

Doyle took a last look around the room, checking every corner for the slightest little detail they might have overlooked, the smallest clue to help them understand what had happened to Peter Lawson.

'Okay, doctor. You've been very helpful. Thank you.'

Bodie said, 'Mind if we look about outside?' He glanced at Doyle, who was pulling a face. They both wondered whether the doctor would be horrified to know of their sprint through the woods and grounds to arrive here, checking on how long it would have taken Lawson to sprint away.

Lowe shook his head, and turned to go. 'Be my guest. But the grounds are huge . . .'

'One more thing,' said Doyle, as Lowe reached the door.

The Major stopped and turned. 'Would you say ... Lawson, is he dangerous?'

Lowe frowned. 'Dangerous?'

'Likely to do harm to his fellow man,' explained Bodie, his voice heavy with sarcasm. Lowe didn't glance at him, but after a moment smiled at Doyle, and cooled the situation. 'Colonel Lawson may have recently been under some strain,' he said. 'But he is still a serving officer in the British Army. And I believe he is aware of that, and will behave accordingly.'

And with that - which answered nothing of Doyle's question - he turned on his heel and left.

Chapter Four

The army base at Grimshot had hardly changed at all in the years since Bodie had done some regulation drilling here, for three months of his life. Protected from the road by a dense stand of ash woodland, and a high, barbed wire fence, the access to the camp was along a winding track (marked 'closed') and thence to the wide, concrete approach road, and the inevitable barricade.

Once beyond the guarded barrier, Bodie felt instantly at home. He pulled the Capri off the main thoroughfare, and let it stand, engine idling, while he surveyed the rows of drab, dark-grey barracks, and the ramshackle Nissen huts, their corrugated iron roofs in bad need of replacement.

The parade ground was wide, and filled with small troop units moving precisely, and efficiently about their business. Two large transports were being loaded with sand bags by tired looking rookies in faded khaki uniforms.

In the distance, a voice could be heard barking out orders.

'Grim looking place,' observed Doyle, peering across his partner at the unfriendly buildings.

'Aptly named, then,' said Bodie. 'But you'd be surprised at how comfortable those huts are.' He looked round at Doyle. 'For a cockroach, that is.'

A convoy of jeeps, plus two small armoured cars, swept in from the outside, and noisily and smokily passed the stationary car, finally vanishing round the huts, nearer to the depots.

'They all look bored out of their minds,' observed Ray Doyle. 'Or frustrated. No local talent, then?'

'I wouldn't say that,' said Bodie, with a typical Bodie knowing grin. 'Not easy to find, but very co-operative when you find it. See that hut there . . . ?' He pointed out one of the more delapidated of the Nissen huts.

'Scene of a great conquest?'

Doyle sensed a disgusting Bodie story coming up, the sort of story that could enliven a stake-out, and make grown agents groan instead of maintaining silence.

'She was twenty-two years old,' said Bodie, 'and she really ought to have know better. I mean, you sneak into an army camp with a twenty-year old private, you really shouldn't expect romance . . .'

'What'd she get?'

'Forty members of C Squad. Culminating in Corporal Evans, known affectionately as Clapper Evans.' Bodie chuckled to himself. 'I bet her ears are still ringing.'

Doyle looked disgustedly at his colleague. 'Save it for the privacy of your own home. Come on, let's get to the Brigadier.

Bodie revved up and swung the car round through the barracks and up to the low, white-washed building that was Company HQ. A stocky, gruff corporal opened the car for them, scowling as he introduced himself as Corporal Pickersgill, and practically snapping orders at them. He led the way to the Brigadier's room, and with a muttered statement of 'Don't need no more bother *today*,' left the two CI5 men to their own devices.

Before either of them could knock at the door to the Brigadier's office, that same door was flung open, and the short, stiffly upright form of Brigadier Tennant emerged, glancing at each of them in turn.

'Ray Doyle,' said Doyle, extending his hand.

'Bodie,' said Bodie.

'Brigadier Tennant,' said the Brigadier, and briefly shook each of the proffered hands. 'Cowley's told me about you. Says you're good men. Says you work hard, and relish danger. Says you're irresponsible louts during your time off. Like the sound of you.'

Bodie and Doyle exchanged meaningful glances. 'I was a cub scout,' said Doyle. 'What could George have meant?'

'Let's walk,' said Tennant, and led the way out into the cool air of the parade ground.

As they strolled round the perimeter of the large, concrete drill area, Doyle briefly accounted for their findings – or rather lack of findings – at Hembury Hospital.

'No sign of a struggle, either in the room, or in the undergrowth at its closest points to Lawson's room. If he'd been kidnapped they'd have had to carry him out of the place. Someone would have noticed. Someone would have heard.'

'So your conclusions are . . .' said Tennant, walking with his hands clasped behind his back, staring at the ground in front of him.

Bodie said, 'He left the hospital under his own steam. He planned and effected the getaway himself.'

'Or was programmed to plan and effect the getaway,' said Doyle, and met Tennant's glance as the Brigadier reacted to that possibility.

'I am frightened, gentlemen, frightened of the possibility that Lawson has defected. I don't mind admitting that. It is a conceivable alternative, and it makes me knot inside to contemplate it. But with the sort of military secrets he *was* privy to, I can't help thinking that the Russians would surely have preferred him to remain under cover. It makes little sense to call him back.'

Bodie and Doyle stopped simultaneously and turned on the Brigadier, who hesitated, nearly stumbled, and looked from one to the other of them.

Bodie said sharply. 'That's very interesting, but a little bit above us . . .'

'The trouble is,' put in Doyle, eqaully forcefully, 'Nobody has told us just exactly what happened to Lawson . . .'

'In Germany,' added Bodie, as Tennant's gaze swung back to him. 'To make the army so uptight that they call in CI5.'

Tennant raised his hands to silence them, then nodded soberly and smiled, smoothing his moustaches as he contemplated his next move.

'I thought you'd come to that. To Germany. I'd hoped that Lawson would turn up, that somehow you'd find him without effort, and without anything having to come out about what happened.'

'Unfortunately,' said Bodie, 'We're working in the dark.'

'We need some illumination,' said Doyle, and fell into step beside Tennant as he wandered on, slapping his swagger stick against his thigh as he strolled.

'All right. Listen carefully, because this is for your ears only . . . and Cowley's . . . and is not to appear in any report, either written or verbal. It may not *sound* like a very serious turn of events to you, but I assure you that the ramifications are terrifying, and unpredictable.

'Last month, NATO forces in Western Europe conducted a very large scale, fully co-ordinated military exercise. Much of this, of course, was done in a glare of publicity, and as you can imagine, what the public saw was just an elaborate game of tin soldiers. The real exercise was conducted in the utmost secrecy, disguised by the play-acting of some fourteen companies. If the English public ever found out what *really* was being trained, and tested, what techniques, what armaments, what special facilities, we'd have every disarmament group in the country breathing down Whitehall's necks.'

Bodie, walking slightly behind the Brigadier, didn't like the sound of that at all, and he met Doyle's backward glance, and shared his partners alarmed expression. Doyle, being impetuous, couldn't help saying, 'I'm not so sure I approve of all this ...'

But Tennant cut him short, with an abrasive, 'It's not up to you to approve or otherwise. You're not given the choice.'

'Fair enough,' said Doyle grimly. CI5 itself operated on the very edge of amorality. But just because their techniques for the country's defence were at the very fringe of legality and responsibility, didn't mean that the Agencies operatives were necessarily in support of military expansion and secrecy.

Tennant went on, 'Lieutenant-Colonel Lawson had an opportunity to try out some new fangled battle plan he had been proposing for a long time. The eyes of the top-brass world wide – the friendly top-brass, that is – they were all on him. And to cut a long story short, the whole scheme went wildly wrong ... a total disaster ...'

From military paranoia to 'new fangled battle plan' was an abrupt defusion of tension that puzzled Bodie. Perhaps Tennant was just another Colonel Blimp after all. 'That's it, is it?' he said, when he realised that Tennant would not continue.

'Sadly no,' said the Brigadier, and Doyle shrugged and added. 'Well what, then? What else?'

Brigadier Tennant stopped and stared across the parade

ground to where the fading light of the day had caused the Nissen Huts to become dark, featureless structures, almost sinister to regard. From one of them came the sound of gunfire, an old weapon being re-primed, no doubt.

'You're both familiar with the way these military exercises are run . . .'

Bodie said. 'Yeah. We've been in a few.'

Tennant went on. 'They have umpires all over the place, tell you how you're doing – whether you're dead or alive, how many tanks you've got left – all computer assisted, of course, probabilities worked out to the Nth place, each soldier a tiny statistic, shuffled between one board and another. Simulation. Very real, very accurate provided everybody plays the game.'

'And did Lawson play the game . . . asked Doyle, leaping ahead of the Brigadier as he began to envision a scenario for chaos.

Tennant looked at him, something of admiration in his steely gaze. 'No he didn't. That's the whole point. When his entire battalion was wiped out – that's eight hundred men – instead of accepting it gracefully – or even ungracefully for that matter – he refused to return to barracks, to turn in his tags. He took his few remaining troops, some in fact who should by rights have been dead, and launched an attack on his own HQ.'

Doyle laughed out loud at that, quite admiring the man's cheek. He fell swiftly silent as he caught Bodie's solemn, pouting look. Bodie could see that such behaviour had been no joke.

'When you say attacked . . . Do you mean, attacked for real?'

Brigadier Tennant seemed to choke on the words, and the CI5 men realised simultaneously that the events involving Lawson had been as much a personal shock for the man, as a military shock.

'I'm afraid I do,' said the Brigadier with difficulty. 'He'd got a regulation issue of live rounds, quite commonplace in a simulation. In the hands of a responsible officer, that edge of danger is very valuable to new recruits. But he killed two men, and severely wounded four others. I can still hardly believe it . . . Knew his father so well, such a grand man . . . Such hopes for his son . . .'

There was a moment's silence, as Tennant seemed to be actively fighting back tears. He had risen to a stiff, attention attitude, hands behind his back, gaze fixed into the distance.

'As it was related to me – he persisted in justifying it all on the grounds of the logic of total warfare, minimum ultimate casualties or whatever . . . I'll never be able to understand it. He was destined for the very top. Highest command. Would have made his father so . . .' He broke off, unwilling to allow himself to sink into maudlin sentiment.

Doyle asked gently. 'Has it totally wrecked his career, then?'

'Absolutely. He's finished. And deep down, he knows it. He must know it. That's what makes him so unpredictable, now. That's why we need you.'

He needed a third man. The mission could not succeed with only two.

Nobby Clarke had hesitated for some time before saying to Lawson, 'I think I know just the man, sir. If you'll trust me, I'll take you to him. You won't be disappointed.'

Lawson was shaved and cleaned; he was fed and wined; he stood tall and spruce in his uniform, the insignia of his rank a proud sight on his epaulets. He turned to face his Sergeant. 'I trust you, Nobby. I'd like to meet him.'

The pleasure that manifested itself in the grizzled face of the old soldier was a sure sign that Nobby Clarke had finally fallen under the spell of his old Colonel.

Half an hour later they approached a ramshackle, green caravan, that was parked at the corner of a fallow field, overlooking some scrubby downland to the south. The trackway was bumpy and pot-holed, and Nobby Clarke steered his battered Cortina through the hazards with an almost desperate look upon his face.

He hit the horn twice as they came up close to the caravan. Lawson, seated stiffly beside him, stared ahead, watching the uninhabited land around, wary for motion that was suspicious.

He was still unarmed. Nobby had not yet relaxed enough to show him the cache of arms he had acquired over the years of his military service.

The door to the caravan opened as Nobby drew the Cortina to a stop and wrenched on the hand-brake. Lawson stepped out of the car, and tried to massage his aching back. Just half an hour on that non-existent suspension had made him feel like a cripple. But he soon straightened up, and let his cold, hard gaze rest on the human phenomenon that stepped down from its tiny home.

Nobby had already warned him that Tug Willis was built like an oak tree. Lawson reflected that he was built more like a mountain than a tree ... The trees were the two, thick trunks that carried the immense body towards him.

Willis, he guessed, was in his forties and, despite his size, he was fit. There was something fluid and controlled in his movement towards the visitors, and when he tucked in his check shirt, Lawson could see the bulge of muscle in arm and stomach.

This was not a fat man. This was a circus strong-man. However ugly Willis's excessive poundage might have been, it was fit and trained, and exploitable.

And Willis had one further feature that did not escape Lawson's scrutiny.

His pugnacious, moronic expression was enough to put the fear of God into an East End hoodlum.

He was just the man for the mission, and Lawson whispered to Nobby, 'I like the look of him.'

Thank you, sir. I reckon he's just the man for you.'

'That,' said Lawson, slightly more coldly. 'We'll soon find out.'

Tug Willis seemed a little confused, which didn't surprise Lawson one bit. The man hesitated when still twenty yards away, wiping his hands on his oil-stained denim jeans. Nobby walked across to him, and patted him on the arm.

'Come and meet the Colonel, Tug.'

Lawson did not see the exaggerated wink that passed between the two men.

Willis ambled over, and stood stiffly to attention before the formidable shape of Lawson; Lawson stood with his hands clasped behind his back, and his legs braced apart.

He stared at Willis, and slowly the look in the big man's eyes blanked as he returned to his long forgotten mode of silent, mindless obedience.

When Willis was totally subjugated to the intense look of authority before him, Lawson snapped out, 'You're Willis.'

Nobby Clarke said. 'They call him Tug, sir. He answers best to Tug.'

'Tug,' repeated Lawson. 'A good name. A strong name.'

'Yeah,' said Tug Willis, exposing three bad teeth, and an expanse of toothless gum. He had smiled slightly, obviously pleased at the flattery.

'And I imagine ... Tug ... that Nobby has fully acquainted you with just who I am, and what I want to do.'

Tug frowned. It was that big word in the middle of the sentence. He glanced at Nobby who gave him a comrade's wink and nod. Tug straightened up, understanding that he was supposed to answer in the affirmative.

'Yeah.'

'I am led to believe, Tug, that you have military experience. That you've been in the army. Is that true?'

'Yessir. Paras. Twelve years. But that was a long time ago.' Again he looked at Nobby, who merely encouraged him. Tug still stood at a stiff attention, his mighty, meaty gut thrust out towards Lawson.

'What rank were you?'

'Corporal. Sir.'

'And what action did you see?'

'Borneo, sir. I was in Borneo ...'

'Where else?'

'Aden, Sir. A year in Aden. And then Cyprus. Following that ... the Sudan. Then Northern Ireland.' He hesitated, let his sunken-eyed gaze meet Lawson's, assessing whether or not he should mention his time as a mercenary. 'And some other places. Don't rightly remember.'

'I understand, Corporal,' said Lawson, relaxing the bulky man by his pure presence and exuded confidence. 'Undercover work, right?'

'Er, yessir. Undercover work.'

Lawson stepped closer to Tug Willis, then slapped him heartily on the arm. 'We need a good man, Tug. I'm looking for a volunteer.'

Tug nodded his head very slightly. He glanced for reassurance at Nobby, who grinned broadly and gave him a nod and a wink.

Tug Willis' blank face split in a wide, contented smile.

Lawson said. 'Stand easy . . . Tug . . .' And, as the big man braced his legs apart, and clasped his hands behind his back in the old military fashion, Lawson added. 'Welcome aboard!'

They returned to Nobby's cafe, and by early evening Tug Willis was so taken by Lawson's commanding presence that he would have followed the officer to the ends of the earth.

In a pub, later, they celebrated the formation of their team of three with beer, and whisky chasers. Willis became drunk very quickly, Nobby Clarke being a little more cuatious with his intake, but still qualifying as semi-paralytic. Lawson drank too. It had been long months since he had last been allowed to. But Lawson drank for the memory of his army days, and for the feeling of euphoria that it gave him.

He did not drink to excess, and did not get drunk, although he was high, very high, on his own spirits!

The time had come to give both Nobby and Tug the first inkling of what they had 'signed up' to do. The situation was perfect. Lawson could tell what sort of a place this noisy public house was, and he could sense the response he would get to a test so simple that it seemed almost pointless.

'I'll tell you what's wrong with this country, shall I?' He said loudly, feigning a greater degree of drunkenness than he actually felt.

Tug swigged on his beer, then nodded vigorously. 'Yeah, Colonel. Tell us.'

Around them a group of farmers were singing noisily, and happily. A crowd was gathered at the bar, jostling for position at the front.

Lawson slammed down his glass and rose to his feet. He stood to attention, hands beside his hips, eyes staring straight ahead. In his wavering baritone, and at the top of his voice, he began to sing the national anthem. He sang it vigorously, if tunelessly, emphasising each beat, and when he reached 'God save the Queen' he practically shouted each word.

By the time he had finished he had managed to reduce the public bar to a hushed, appalled silence. All eyes were on him. Even the bar staff had stopped pouring drinks and were watching him, ready for trouble, ready to get the police if this boisterous man got out of control.

Lawson looked around him with arrogant non-concern. He sneered at the patrons, shaking his head, then turning triumphantly to Tug and Nobby. 'You see what's wrong with them? You see? They don't stand!' Again he looked around, and practically shouted, 'Not one of them stood! They don't stand to their own national anthem!'

Now he was angry, really angry. He had intended to use the cultural rudeness of the pub's customers as an illustration of what was lacking in the country, but he had managed to incense himself, to drive himself close to the edge of fury.

His eyes blazed. His face burned. He was dizzy, more than ever determined to teach these people a lesson, a lesson they would never forget.

He leaned down towards Nobby Clarke, who was trying to focus upon him, but was clearly unable to. The fumes of drink were rich, almost stunning.

Lawson put his arm round Nobby's shoulder, and reached out to touch Tug Willis affectionately on the arm.

'We're going to fight, my men. We're going to fight for this country's . . . eternal soul . . .'

And solemnly he raised his glass, drinking a toast to a salvation that he was confident would come.

Around them, the atmosphere of the bar returned to normal.

The house was quite obviously Georgian, but had been considerably renovated and re-faced in the early nineteen hundreds, so that now it was an ugly mixture of two cultures. It seemed large and grey, a gaunt building that held the promise of long, silent rooms, and the dusty playground of many a ghost.

On two sides this family seat of the Lawson family was crowded by yew and birch trees; to the front, however, there was a wide, gravel approach that led to a terraced garden, magnificently landscaped.

George Cowley drove slowly along the winding roadway, and parked on the gravel forecourt. He stepped from the car and stretched, then walked across to the steps down to the gardens and spent a minute or two admiring the meticulously planned rose and flower beds. There was an air of welcome tranquility about the place, and it was an ideal balm to Cowley's own feelings of tension. It helped him compose himself prior to the meeting to come, during which he would have to be on his guard; a meeting that would require both diplomacy and care.

At length he turned to the house, and unbuttoned his dark great-coat, walking swiftly up to the massive oak doorway and ringing the bell.

The woman who answered was hollow eyed and drawn, a human spectre clad in plain, but clearly expensive clothes. Her hand shook as she greeted Cowley, her mouth twitched in an uncertain smile.

'Do come in,' she said. 'I'm a little disordered at the moment. There's one of those wretched flu bugs going round, and most of my staff are off sick.'

'I shan't keep you long, Mrs Lawson. Thank you for seeing me.'

Cowley followed her into the house, still quite disturbed by her frailty, and awful vulnerability. She seemed to his pragmatic northern eyes to be a woman suffering from solitude; her husband dead, her children gone from home, and rarely in contact. It would probably kill her to know what had happened to Peter, he thought, and despite his years of training in bottling up emotion, Cowley felt a frisson of depression for the gallant old lady.

The lounge to which Lavina Lawson conducted the CI5 man was quite immense, but a group of beautiful old settees had been gathered together round the open fire, making a room within the room. The walls were covered with family portraits and weapons in a display similar, on a much smaller scale, to the sort of display of family antiquities that could be found in any stately home. Cowley walked around the room, admiring, commenting, and quite genuinely enjoying this brief insight into the shape and career of the famous military family.

'We've lived here now for nearly two hundred years,' said

Mrs Lawson as she followed the appreciative Cowley on his slow ambling tour.

'A most impressive collection,' said the Scot. He pointed to a wide-stocked flintlock, its barrel nearly eight feet long. 'Afghanistan, I see ...'

'My great grandfather, Thomas Lawson. he died there ...'

'China ... Tibet ... Burma ... the Light Brigade is that?'

He was looking at a picture of a slim young man in the tight britches and jacket of a mid-nineteenth-century horse soldier. The arrogance in the young man's eyes was appalling, almost radiant. The face, with its thin, cold lips, and half-lidded, uncaring stare was very reminiscent of the image of Peter Lawson. Two of a kind, Cowley thought, and that idle reflection was confirmed when Lavinia Lawson said, 'That's right. He didn't participate in the infamous charge, but he had a commission in the Crimea. We don't talk very much about Harry. The black sheep of the family. Used the war front to line his own pockets, with a group of cavalry men, all working class. I suppose you'd call them mercenaries these days ...'

'There has to be one,' observed George Cowley, walking away from the portrait.

They chatted for a while, and Cowley repeated his story that he had been in Malaya with James Lawson – Lavinia's husband – for some years. Although he had been back in England on occasion, he said, it was only now that he had returned here to settle again, and he had felt the compulsion to visit James' old home, to touch, however briefly, the memory of a good friend.

Lavinia Lawson had been delighted to invite him round.

'It's strange, though,' she said, as they sat in the deep sofa, close to the empty fire place, 'He never mentioned you in any of his letters. Mind you, he never mentioned many people at all. It was always descriptions of country, and long diatribes about inefficiency ...'

Cowley laughed. 'I remember those all right.'

Mrs Lawson considered the elegant man seated close to her, feeling relaxed with Cowley, glad of his company. 'Were you in Malaya with him when he actually died?'

'No. I was transferred shortly before. I didn't find out for some time, to tell you the truth.'

Mrs Lawson nodded, understanding. 'Army duties. No time for compassion in war.'

She stood and went to the marble mantelpiece, where a group photograph was almost hidden behind other trophies and mementoes of her earlier life.

She studied the photograph for a moment, then passed it to Cowley. 'It was taken at the Mess . . . to think . . . as he sat there smiling so brightly, he only had a week left on this earth.'

Cowley looked appropriately solemn, but Mrs Lawson had spoken simply, factually, unsentimentally. 'I wasn't there for the photograph,' he said. 'But tell me, how is young . . . Peter, isn't it? James told me much about him.'

Mrs Lawson's face brightened at the mention of her son. 'James hardly knew him, really. But I suppose he built up a picture of how he hoped the boy would turn out.'

'He must be - how old now?'

'Nearly forty!'

Cowley feigned disbelief. 'Really! How time flies.'

Lavinia Lawson smiled thinly. 'Ridiculous isn't it. Quite ridiculous. My little Peter, old enough to have a grown family of his own.' She hesitated a moment, and Cowley was about to keep her on the subject, fearing that she might go off at a tangent to avoid the fact that her son had never married (a fact that Cowley suspected was painful to her) when Lavinia Lawson went on, 'He's in Germany now, with his own regiment. He's a Lieutenant-Colonel, and is deeply involved with intelligence. He can't talk much about his work . . .'

'But he keeps in touch?'

Mrs Lawson nodded vigorously. 'Oh yes, certainly. He writes, and he calls me at least once a month. As a matter of fact, he called me only last week.'

From the hospital, thought Cowley. How the hell did he get access to a phone? The man was supposed to have been under observation, secure, guarded . . . 'Oh?' he said, and tried to look like a man interested, hoping to prompt Mrs Lawson to expound on that call.

She took his simple, social bait.

'He wanted to trace some old sergeant who'd been under

his command once . . . Seems like everybody wants to pick up on the past at the moment.'

'Indeed!' said Cowley with an affectionate smile.

'This particular man,' went on Mrs Lawson, 'Had written a letter at Christmas, wanting advice on whether to get married. Isn't it funny how those tough men are like children. They look to their officers for anything, even after they've left the army . . .'

'Yes . . .' said Cowley.

'Peter had lost the letter, but it didn't take me long to find out where the man lived.'

Cowley felt a thrill of excitement as he realised that he was the first real break that CI5 had got in the case of Peter Lawson. It was the work of moments to find out the name and address of Lawson's contact, and Lavinia Lawson never suspected for a moment the use that she had been to the government agency.

Cowley rapidly made his excuses, thanked her for her hospitality, and made his way out of the imposing old house and into the bright day.

He went straight to his car, and flicked on his R/T. 'Alpha One to control,' he said, and didn't have to repeat the call before control answered with a crackling, 'Come in Alpha.'

'Message for 3.7 and 4.5. Target may have contracted former army colleague Len Clarke, runs cafe in Cornbrook.'

'Copy you, Alpha One. Out.'

Crowley flicked off the R/T. He could see Lavinia Lawson watching him from an upstairs window, and when she caught his eyes she waved delicately. Cowley waved back.

'There has to be *one*,' he said to himself. 'There always has to be one . . .'

'I'd quite fancied a plate of egg and chips,' said Ray Doyle sadly, 'Until I saw that place.'

He and Bodie were still seated in their Capri, parked now by the side of the narrow main street of Cornbrook. They were twenty yards from Nobby's dirty-looking cafe.

'Can't do much decorating if you only sell five cups of tea a day,' observed Bodie. 'Must have had better trade once.'

'Before the motorway, I suppose. Places like this used to be sure-fire quality grub-houses. Now they rip you off at every turn.'

'Could do with a cup of tea, though.'

'Come on then.'

Doyle swung out of the car and slammed the door. He led the way to the cafe, and pushed into the hot, rather fishy smelling interior.

There were three customers, two of them tucking into chips and beans, the third an old lady sipping a cup of tea and reading a magazine. None of them looking up as Bodie and Doyle came in. Nobody, that is, except the waitress.

She was a full chested girl, with curly blonde hair, and far too much make-up. And she was obviously delighted with the looks of the two new arrivals.

Her gaze darted between the two of them as they approached the counter, but her interest was mainly fixed on Bodie's smooth, boyish features; Bodie saw this, gave Ray Doyle a knowing glance, and moved in close.

Doyle grinned, and propped himself against the counter, glancing round the cafe at the three customers. 'Is Nobby around, love?' Bodie asked casually.

Doreen leaned on the counter, shoulders forward so that her blouse opened and her cleavage deepened. Bodie didn't fail to notice Doreen's generous proportions and let his eyes linger there for a moment, before looking up sharply, with a smile on his face, saying, 'We've come to see him.'

The girl's eyelashes fluttered. 'Friends of his, are you?'

'Not exactly,' said Ray Doyle. 'Friends of a friend . . . With a message. Is he in, then?'

Doreen shook her head. She looked angry for a moment, then softened. 'No. He's not been around all morning. Left me to manage the place all on my own.'

'Not too busy,' said Bodie. 'Sure you can manage.'

Doreen looked girlish. 'I could do with a hand. If you know what I mean.'

Bodie said, keeping the girl's resistance low, 'I'll see what we can do,' and Doyle prompted, 'Where is he . . . Working? Or what?'

'Working!' Doreen looked disgusted. 'He's off playing games.'

'Oh yeah,' said Bodie, and walked round the counter to stand next to her. Doreen fluttered with excitement and didn't notice Bodie's slick, professional glance into the back room of the cafe. 'What sort of games would they be, then?'

He was almost touching her. Ray Doyle watched fascinated as Doreen came so close to the range of Bodie's external hormones that she practically lost control. 'Not the kind of games I'd like to play with you,' she said, and Doyle winced, and turned his head away, trying to stifle his smirk.

Bodie behaved better. He'd sensed that for Doreen there was very little chance of her ever getting away from this backwoods town, and this dead end job. Despite her gaudy, sexy looks, she clearly lacked the initiative to make the break to a big town like London. Or perhaps she knew, intuitively, that if she did head for the smoke she'd only end up being exploited, and that was worse than being chained to a restaurant.

Ray Doyle drew her attention back to him, away from Bodie. 'Come on, dear, where can we find him?'

When her eyes left Bodie's slim form, Bodie took a second, longer look through into the store-room, then walked round the counter again, pinching one of Doreen's well formed buttocks to her utter delight. 'He's out with that Mad Colonel . . .' she said, watching as Bodie rejoined his partner. 'Can I get you anything at all? Tea? Coffee?'

'No ta, love,' said Doyle. 'Just tell us where the Mad Colonel is likely to be. It's really important that we find Nobby . . .'

'Will you come back afterwards?'

Bodie gave her a wink. 'Of course. We'll be here quite a lot, I should think.'

Doreen said, 'I don't know exactly where they'll be. But most likely they'll be out by the golf course. That's west, about two miles.'

'Thanks,' said Doyle, and stood up straight, shaking his tousled hair as he watched Bodie still giving the girl the eye. 'That's enough now,' he muttered as he walked to the door. 'Anybody would think you're an actor.'

Doyle took the wheel, spun the car round in the narrow street, and accelerated out of Cornbrook like the proverbial bat leaving hell. Bodie waved at Doreen's pale features, still watching them from the cafe.

They drove swiftly along the winding country road, enjoying the exaggerated sense of speed that the close-by trees and hedges gave to the car's progress. Bodie clung on to the dashboard for dear life.

'What's the hurry?'

'Need some action,' said Doyle grimly. 'Too much talk, too much sitting around. If there's something to Lawson other than an escaped looney, let's get on with it.'

Bodie nodded solemnly. 'Couldn't agree with you more.'

They spotted the golf-club notice more or less where Doreen had indicated the golf course lay; Doyle swung the car violently off the road and onto a rough dirt track that skirted the vast expanse of lush green turf, and rolling hillocks. 'Just drive?' he said, and Bodie grunted.

They would have to scan a large area. There was nothing else for it than to drive fast, and cover as much ground as possible.

But they were in luck. Within five minutes, some way from the sight of the golf course, they saw a battered old car parked, half hidden, among some trees. Beyond the trees was an embankment.

They stopped some way away and jumped from the car, running in their best crouched way up the embankment, to fall belly flat at the top, peering over.

Doyle had already heard the distant sound of a man's voice, shouting orders.

In the distance, on a patch of scrub-land bordering a small, newly planted stand of fir trees, three figures marched about in the stiff, goose-stepping gait of toy soldiers. Shouted commands drifted on the breeze. The figures wheeled and marched, swung their arms, and turned about.

'What the devil's that?' said Doyle, his rugged features craggier than ever as he squinted into the distance.

'Colonel Blimp,' said Bodie nonchalantly. His heavy hand-gun seemed suddenly to become a ludicrous presence in his right hand and he slipped it back into his holster. Doyle reached into the pocket of his short leather windcheater and drew out a monocular, extended it to its full length and peered, in close up, at the distant trio of figures.

'Lawson's there all right. He's putting two men through their paces . . . the small one must be Clarke. The other guy looks mean.'

'How mean?' asked Bodie casually.

'Rib-crushing mean,' answered Doyle. Meaning, thick but violent.

'No sweat,' said Bodie. 'I don't recognise the weapons . . .'

The three figures had weapons over their shoulders. From this distance they looked like small rifles. But Ray Doyle snickered as he passed the monocular to Bodie, his pugnacious face filled with humour.

'What calibre, d'you think?' he asked, as Bodie grinned thinly.

'Depends what trees they cut them from,' said Bodie.

Doyle ran back down the embankment to the parked Capri, reached in for the R/T, and used it as he stood, leaning against the roof, still watching Bodie's spread-eagled form at a distance.

'4.5 to Control. Relay to Alpha.'

After a moment the voice of control crackled back that the relay was through.

'Come in Alpha one.'

And Cowley's gruff voice bellowed out of the handset, 'Alpha One. Go ahead, 4.5.'

'Your lead was correct! We've found Lawson about two miles from Cornbrook.'

'Good work, 4.5,' rasped Cowley. His voice was interrupted by sounds of traffic, and Doyle guessed that the chief was driving somewhere in crowded West London. 'How is he?'

'Where shall I start?' said Doyle. 'He certainly hasn't defected . . . and there's not much danger of him being kidnapped.'

'What do you mean by that, 4.5? Make yourself clear man.'

'From the look of things, I don't think the Russian's would want him!'

Up on the embankment, Bodie beckoned to his partner,

and Doyle trotted back to the observation position, keeping Cowley waiting at the other end of the communication line.

Mock bayonet attacks were in process in the distance, and it looked so funny that even solemn Bodie was being reduced to a flicker of mirth.

Cowley's voice was tinged with irritation as he demanded for perhaps the third time,'4.5, 3.7. Could you be a little more specific?'

Bodie reached out for the R/T, as he passed Doyle's monocular back. 'This is 3.7. Is this specific enough? The Colonel is bananas. Repeat, the Colonel is bananas.'

Ray Doyle was grinning as he scanned the distant shape of the Mad Colonel. Cowley was not amused.

'Are you saying he's mad, 3.7?'

'Off his rocker,' said Bodie. 'And 4.5 would agree with me,' Doyle nodded, 'That he seems quite harmless. Doing a bit of square bashing with two other blokes, and tree branches for weapons. Perhaps they're going to steal apples.'

There was a long silence from Cowley's end. Then the chief's voice growled. 'Right. Give his position to control and I'll have Brigadier Tennant advised immediately. You boys get back to HQ. We'll find you some real work.'

Bodie cut the connection, and he and Doyle slipped quickly down the embankment and back to the car. 'Which is the quickest way back to London?' said Bodie, as he slipped into the driver's seat.

'Via Bristol,' said Doyle. 'And a little steak bar and night club I know there.'

'Jolly good show,' said Bodie, and span the Capri, with a squeal of its suspension, in a tight circle and back the way they had come.

The Colonel is bananas . . .

The Colonel is off his rocker!

The Colonel is harmless . . .

How those words would have pleased Lieutenant-Colonel Peter Lawson had he heard them. How amused he would have been, had he had such a thing as a sense of humour, to have listened to Bodie and Doyle's whispered reports to George Cowley.

What a triumph of irony he would have experienced.

He entered the bank ahead of Tug Willis and Nobby Clarke, but he felt their rushed arrival behind him, saw them split up and run to different ends of the queueing area. 'NOBODY MOVE!' bellowed Lawson, and Tug struck one arrogant youth with the butt of his FN automatic rifle, knocking the boy back against the counter from which he had been about to run.

'Stand still and you'll not be hurt. Move and you're dead!'

The bank froze, customers, tellers, clerking staff, all of them became as statues, staring across the space at the violent, grotesque forms that were invading them.

They wore black balaclavas, commando style, with army berets above. Their clothes were the black skin-suits of the SAS, tight belted, with weaponry and gadgets slung from those belts in profusion. From behind the featureless mask of the leader, grey, ice-cold eyes glittered with triumph, passion and madness.

'*Now* you move!' barked Lawson. 'To the wall, all of you. Hands on heads, mouths closed, eyes closed. MOVE!'

As the bemused customers herded across to Tug Willis, that stocky ex-soldier clubbed, and jostled them into submission. They huddled, terrified, by the west wall, not knowing whether to be more frightened of the stiff, arrogant figure in the centre of the bank, or the grotesque giant whose laboured breathing and dulled eyes were the only real features they could tell about him.

Tug Willis sounded like an ape, ready to break bones . . . ready to discharge his deadly automatic at the slightest whimper.

Nobby Clarke was admitted by a terrified young girl teller to the till-space behind the bullet-proof grilles. Lawson walked forward two paces, slipped his own sub-machine gun, a British Stirling, with two banana clips taped together at the side, through the small, delivery space of one of the counters. He pointed the barrel at the fat, bearded manager who was sitting, hands elevated, at the back of the bank.

Nobby began to collect the cash from the tills, holding his sawn-off shotgun towards the cashiers, using his right hand to scoop notes into a leather bag dangling from his belt.

There had to be a hero of course. His name was David Wingrove.

He couldn't have been more than eighteen, probably only been working there a few months. In his natty, grey suit, with his hair in meticulous modern trim, his face smooth, still almost beardless, no doubt he was thinking more of the charisma it would give him to be a hero, than of the consequences of wrestling with a discharge of twelve bore lead.

He made a dive for the alarm switch.

At eighteen years of age a man is immortal. Death is meaningless. He might get hurt, he might fail, but the idea of being blown away just never occurred to him . . .

'Sergeant!' yelled Lawson. 'Stop that man! STOP HIM!'

Nobby whipped his shotgun round, two hands on the breech, stock against his hip to take the recoil.

The boy's fingers were inches from the alarm button when the blast of one barrel struck him from head to chest and blew him, flew him, spread him across the farther wall of the bank. His jacket caught on a shelf and the grotesque, headless body dangled there, a horrifying warning to the rest of the staff.

The Colonel was playing soldiers . . .

Chapter Five

The video room at the end of CI5's section of the Home Office was cool and airy, but at the moment the temperatures were running high, heat generated by irritation and self-disgust.

Cowley, Bodie and Doyle sat, grouped around the twenty-four inch screen, watching the fuzzy black and white images of three men holding up a bank. One of the raiders was tall and lean, another was a giant of a man; the third was short and stocky. All three were dressed in black commando gear, with balaclava face masks, but even so, it was clear enough who they were. The strange, stiff, goose-stepping style of the leader was a characterising detail that was unmistakable.

The tape played through twice. The death of the teller happened off screen, but the smoke that drifted into view afterwards was evidence enough of the violence.

George Cowley watched the raid, caught on the bank's security cameras, with impassive silence. When the tape had been played twice he continued to stare at the screen thoughtfully, then turned to the two youthful men beside him.

Bodie and Doyle didn't meet his gaze. They were both solemn, both unkempt, still dressed in tight, faded jeans and zipped up windcheaters.

After a moment Cowley said, 'Well?'

Bodie looked round at him, his smooth, strong features twisted into a moment's self-disgust. His full lipped mouth pouted with indignation, a very Bodie gesture.

'Yeah,' he said. 'That's them all right. No doubt about it. That's them.'

Doyle nodded his curly-haired head, his wide blue eyes narrowed slightly. 'No question.'

George Cowley regarded his two top agents carefully, his craggy features giving little away as to the thoughts that were going through his mind. 'What specifically is it that you recognise about them, Bodie? The harmlessness?'

Bodie said, glumly, 'The bananas.'

'They're crazy,' said Doyle, shaking his head, trying to inject some proper indignation into his voice. 'To think they could get away with something as blatant as this, they must be crazy!'

Cowley said stiffly, 'I'm not so sure about that.'

Bodie and Doyle exchanged a querulous glance, then stared at their chief. Cowley said. 'That peculiar way of walking, like Russian marching, that went a long way to forming your own decision that they were ... off their rockers, I think was the expression Bodie used. But we've identified a lot of individuals simply by their walk, their characteristic gait. Even by the way they've stood.'

Doyle saw the light. 'I get it. This goosestepping is a form of disguise.'

'Possibly,' said Cowley, and Bodie butted in, 'I *don't* get it. They've given themselves away with their funny walks just the same as if they hadn't bothered.'

'They didn't know they'd been observed, remember,' added Cowley softly.

'They still couldn't keep walking like that all the time,' the younger man persisted, and Doyle grinned and added, 'Unless they want to lie low in the Moscow Mayday Parade.'

Cowley cut into what promised to be a lightening of a desperately serious mood. 'Enough levity, gentlemen. A man is dead because of these crazy soldiers. Don't forget that.'

Doyle winced, feeling the guilt of negligence weighing heavy on his shoulders. 'How much did they get?'

'About eighteen thousand,' said Cowley matter-of-factly.

Bodie leaned forward in his chair, hands clasped before him, brow furrowed. 'I don't get it ...'

'You still don't get it?' said Doyle with a twinkle of humour directed at his colleague. Bodie ignored him. 'Eighteen thousand is chicken feed. Lawson was rich, right? He could cash a cheque for eighteen thousand pounds and not raise eyebrows. Why bother to rob a bank? Why not ring up his broker and sell a few shares?'

Cowley shrugged casually. 'That's a good question. I'll look forward to hearing your answer ...'

He was cut off by the shrill ringing of the inter-office phone. He snatched the grey receiver up and listened intently for a moment. 'Yes ... thank you.'

To Bodie and Doyle he said, 'Right. The Essex Police have found Clarke's car.'

'Essex!' said Doyle vehemently. 'Christ, *they've* moved. What's their game, I wonder?'

'Lawson's a pro,' said Cowley. 'He's probably got hundreds of fox-holes, all over the country. The car was abandoned near a town called Huddespit, which is a long way from anywhere civilised. So I don't recommend that you spend too long looking around on the off-chance.'

Ray Doyle noted all this calmly. He and Bodie had tackled more unlikely, and unpromising, chases. He knew, from long experience, that theirs was a lucky team ... That something would turn up.

'What about the third guy, that giant?' he asked. 'He was carrying an FN automatic. Ulster service, you reckon?'

Cowley shook his head. 'If he'd been in Ulster he'd have known better than to take an FN automatic on a bank raid. You can see on the tape, the man's finding the weapon far too unwieldy. No, I don't think he's had that much experience in recent years. In fact we know who he is, or think we do. According to police interrogation of the girl Doreen who works at Clarke's cafe, his name's Willis, and he's an ex-para.'

'Gone to seed,' said Bodie, thinking of the bulk of the man.

'Maybe,' said Cowley. 'But dangerous. He worked as a bouncer at a caravan camp. If it *is* the same Willis who features on our computer, then he's not shy of action. Military Cross in Aden, earned for wiping out an entire guerilla platoon single handed.'

'Probably bare-handed,' observed Ray Doyle wryly.

Bodie added that, 'If they decided to go into banking like that, they could become quite a successful little firm.'

Doyle rubbed his eyes, trying to banish some of the weariness he felt. 'He certainly said goodbye to a military career.'

Bodie let a characteristic smirk touch his lips. 'I don't know. Looks like he's started another one. From scratch.'

The forest was peaceful and quiet, hardly a bird sound, hardly a breath of wind. It was this silent isolation that had appealed to Lawson when he had first discovered the woodland location, during a private training session some years before. The road was not far away, and yet no one ever stopped and explored this densely thicketed patch of natural countryside. There were no farms that were close enough to bother with smoke, no gypsy encampments to harass them with dogs.

In a wide clearing, Lawson had made his new HQ. They had abandoned Nobby Clarke's battered old Cortina some miles away, and Lawson's intuitive sense of strategy had spotted that any search would occur away from this particular part of the country. With Tug Willis's ex-British Army jeep, a run down, cantankerous, but still functioning, vehicle, they had managed to tow a locally bought caravan into hiding.

The small mobile home was now neatly camouflaged at the edge of the clearing. The whole clearing itself had been organised with the meticulous efficiency of the British Army, or of a scout troop. Tug and Nobby would now share a two man tent, and this was pitched away from the trees – though covered with twigs and turves to hide it from aerial view – facing the south to avoid the plagues of midges that would emerge at sunset. The fire burned hot, fierce and practically smokeless in a deep pit, with the cooking pots slung above it by a neat arrangement of branches. A clothes line was hung between trees, and their change of clothes was drying rapidly. They had a designated food area, campaign area, and relaxation area. The forest clearing was like a miniature army base.

And from the air it would hardly be noticed.

Colonel Lawson was seated in a folding chair, ticking off items on a clipboard, while Nobby squatted on his haunches nearby. Tug Willis was still eating, his third helping of rabbit stew vanishing into his maw in great serving-spoonfuls.

Lawson said, 'Item. Officers Quarters, HQ and mess, fifteen hundred pounds.'

Nobby grinned at the terminology, and ticked off the caravan on his own list, with an officiously grunted, 'Check.'

Lawson went on coldly, efficiently, 'Item. Barracks facilities, temporary. One hundred pounds.'

Nobby checked the tent, felt a bit grim as he thought of squeezing into that with Tug Willis. 'Check,' he said, and wondered why they couldn't have bought a bigger caravan, or at least, *two* tents.

'Item,' said the seated Lawson. 'Transport vehicle and locomotive support, acquired from platoon. Compensation of three hundred pounds.'

'Check,' said Nobby, glancing at the jeep. Again, he wondered why they couldn't have bought a second-hand car, with room in it for them, their weapons, and any other equipment. A jeep was so noticeable, an attention-getter.

'Item. Communications equipment, R/T. Short wave radio. Television. Extra batteries. Transformers. Electrical sundries. Nine hundred pounds.'

Nobby touched each item on the pile close to him, checking them off.

Lawson went on to list their food and drink supplies, and essential toiletries and items of refreshment. The whole lot had come to one hundred and twenty five pounds, and Nobby Clarke had kept receipts for everything. Clothing was next, summer uniforms, winter clothing, parkas, boots, gloves, including specialist items like running-shoes.

Everything was present and correct. The team was equipped, and in style.

'Well Sergeant,' said Lawson eventually, 'What do you add all that up to?'

'Including future food budget, the whole lot totals four thousand, eight hundred and seventy five pounds.'

'Check,' said Lawson. 'Now. Balance of income after expenditures?'

Nobby stood up and went to fetch the canvas bags, into which their stolen money had already been sorted.

'Thirteen thousand pounds and, er . . . forty eight quid.'

Lawson scribbled that down, then nodded, and looked up. 'Very well. Sergeant, you may divide the shares among the men.'

He himself folded up the sheet of paper on which he had been writing, placed it into a buff envelope, and sealed it. As Nobby passed Tug's canvas bag of cash across to the still-eating third member of the party, he glanced quizzically at his Colonel and asked, 'What was that, if you don't mind my asking, sir?'

'This, Nobby,' said Lawson patiently, 'Is a receipt, signed by me, for requisition on behalf of Her Majesty's land forces, which I shall post to the headquarters of the bank.'

Tug Willis had finished eating. Still holding his metal platter he rose to his feet, wiped his sleeve across his mouth, and joined Nobby by the Colonel. He gave Nobby Clarke a worried, curious look, which his friend shared.

Nobby decided that it was time he and Tug received some extra clarification. He was quite sure that Colonel Lawson knew what he was doing, and there was no question of disobedience. He and Tug would have followed the Colonel round the world now, and he had killed that man at the bank without thought and without remorse. The Colonel had said that it was 'for England' and that was good enough for Nobby.

But just where this mission was leading, that wasn't clear at all, and it was an omission from their briefing that was beginning to nag.

'Excuse me, sir, but I think it's time for a word or two.'

Lawson had been standing near the wood fire, hands in his tunic pocket, gazing absently out across the clearing. He turned slowly to face his men.

'What is it, Sergeant?'

'We were wondering ...' Nobby stuttered, uncomfortable beneath Lawson steel-eyed gaze, 'We were wondering, that is, the men ... Whether it mightn't make sense, military wise that is, if we sort of split up for a bit. Depending on whether or not that's appropriate for the mission ...'

Lawson was astonished. 'Split up? That would be a most foolish thing to do, Sergeant. Our mission is only just beginning. Only phase one has been completed. Split up, indeed! No, Nobby. We stick together. It's essential ...'

Tug Willis lurched forward, saluted, and rather sheepishly asked, 'That's just it, sir. We don't know what the mission is, and perhaps ...'

Nobby cut in, 'Perhaps if you filled us in a bit more we wouldn't get so anxious about proper military procedure.'

Lawson surveyed his two men for a long, lingering, thoughtful moment. Yes. They were restless, he could see that now. He should have sensed it before. These men were too long away from the blind, mindless obedience of the barracks to have kept them in the dark through Stage One of the mission.

He would have to throw them a bone, a fragment of information. He would have to simultaneously whet and appease their appetites. He couldn't tell them everything, yet; they wouldn't be able to handle the knowledge of the end of the mission, the final move, the move that would checkmate England in the elaborate game of chess he was playing with the government.

'Very well, men,' he said, as authoritatively as possible. 'Stand at ease.'

Nobby and Tug, who had been shambling about, responded to that instruction as dogs to a dinner bell. They pulled themselves erect, then relaxed into the standard 'at ease' position, legs apart, hands behind backs, eyes fixed hard on their swaggering Colonel.

Lawson played the scene to the utmost, walking up and down in front of them twice, as if collecting his thoughts, then stopping and abruptly turning to face them.

'Men, we are presently engaged in Operation Britannica.' His voice was loud, and he enunciated the words clearly and confidently. Nobby and Tug nodded, as if in agreement, hanging on to every morsel that emerged from Lawson's pale lips.

'Operation Britannica consists of three clear and distinct stages. Stage One, what we might call the funding part of the operation, is already completed. You have all performed extremely well. Stage Two will be a further operation of requisition ...'

'Another bank sir?' butted in Tug Willis, and felt immediately embarrassed as Lawson turned on him.

But Lawson's expression softened and he said, 'No, not another bank ...'

'It's just that that bloke who was killed, sir ...'

Lawson knew how his men felt about that, especially Nobby who had fired the fatal shot. 'Tragic, as I've already said, Tug. But in the line of duty.'

'But a civilian . . .' persisted Tug. 'Soldiers is one thing . . .'

'There'll be no more individual civilians killed, Tug. Nobby. That I guarantee. There won't have to be. Stage Two is a requisition operation . . . Against the army barracks at Offenden. This will be followed by Stage Three, in which we will go for the Big One. From that point on there will only be some final tidying up to do, and then the platoon will be disbanded.'

He stopped talking. He had told them very little more than they already knew, but he had dropped the hint that their final goal was something big, something impressive. He added, 'Are there any questions, men?'

Tug Willis, more confident now that he had spoken out of turn and not been silenced for it, said, 'Yeah. This Big One. How big is that going to be?'

Colonel Lawson smiled and slapped him on the shoulder. 'Bigger, Tug, than anything you could even imagine.'

Tug Willis's eyes widened, and his face slackened into an expression of amazement . . . He may not have been able to imagine Stage Three, but he was certainly trying.

Nobby's cafe was closed when Ray Doyle skidded the car up onto the pavement outside, and jumped from the driver's seat before the engine had hardly ceased turning over.

Bodie, grim faced and angry, got out from the passenger seat and walked across to the cafe door, knocking on it very hard.

Hands in his windcheater, Doyle shook his curly hair out of his eyes as the stiff breeze ruffled it; he stared about the high street, seeing how much attention they had drawn to themselves.

After a few minutes, Doreen appeared at the door, peered through and immediately smiled. Bodie smiled back, waved his hand and indicated that he wanted to come in. Doreen smoothed down her short skirt, and shook back her blonde hair, as she unlocked the yale security lock.

She was taken by surprise at the violence with which Bodie entered her premises. 'Easy, lover boy,' she said, and cried out as Bodie grabbed her by the arm and forced her across the cafe floor to the counter. 'What's going on?' she wheedled, looking away from Bodie to where Ray Doyle sauntered casually across to her, blue eyes expressionless, mouth twitching into a sort of half smile, the sort of expression that was unfathomable and could have meant either humour or deep, deep anger.

'Where's Nobby?' he asked.

'Who are you?' said Doreen again, and jerked her arm away from Bodie's grip, buttoning up her blouse to cover her full cleavage, unhappy, now, with these two young men's scrutiny.

'CI5 darling,' said Doyle, and flashed his ID. 'That's like secret service, if you understand. So don't stand on ceremony. Tell us everything you know about Nobby, and this Colonel Lawson.'

'But I don't know anything!' whined Doreen. 'Look, this is supposed to be my day off, and I've got things to do. Bloody Nobby's vanished, and I don't know whether to open up, or just go shopping. I don't know anything . . .'

Ray Doyle gave Bodie the glance that meant, ease off a little with the hostility, she probably doesn't know much, and we run the risk of losing even that. Bodie backed off accordingly, reached out and gave Doreen an affectionate pat on her well proportioned rump. 'Sorry, love. Got a bit strung up. Lawson's dangerous, and we've got to find him. Nobby is our only chance.'

'Dangerous!' Now Doreen looked worried. 'How dangerous?'

'Don't know exactly,' said Ray Doyle, coming close to Doreen on the other side. She was potently doused with perfume and his nostrils wrinkled. Should he tell her that Nobby was the one who'd pulled the trigger in the bank, or should he keep that quiet? He realised that he didn't know exactly what the relationship between the girl and the ex-soldier was. 'What's Nobby to you?' he asked, with characteristic Doyle bluntness. 'Boyfriend? Or just Boss?'

Doreen looked at him sullenly, obviously unhappy about having to admit what she then admitted. 'We're going to get married. Eventually. One day. Bloody Nobby, says something one day, then changes his mind. He was married before, that's the trouble. He doesn't trust me enough.'

'Then we'd better get him back here quick,' said Ray Doyle with a half smile on his round face, his eyes twinkling, 'Before my friend here gets carried away.'

Bodie let humour touch his lips, but he couldn't banish every vestige of the irritation he still felt at having been raked over Cowley's coals.

Doreen had relaxed some more, still glancing with approval at Bodie's handsome features, at his tight jeans and the casual thrust of his hip as he leaned on the counter.

'That's right, love,' Bodie said. 'I might just sling you over my shoulder. Carry you away from all this.'

Doreen laughed cynically. 'Wouldn't take much to get me away from this lot, I can tell you.'

She led the way round the counter, and into the back room, which was a store room. From here, a rickety stairs led up to a primitively furnished, but comfortable living space. 'More comfortable to talk here,' she said. and as Bodie began to mooch around the room, picking up objects, photographs, peering into drawers, Doyle sat with the girl and prompted her further.

'You must have heard Nobby talking. Did they mention any names, any other names? Any places?'

'Tug Willis,' said Doreen. 'I heard them talking about Tug . . . He lives nearby . . .'

Bodie said from across the room. 'We all know about Willis. Any other names? Places?'

'Apart from going out to the golf course, no . . .'

Doyle patted her hand. 'Where are they now, any idea?'

Doreen looked distressed again. 'No. They just upped and went, yesterday, real early. Nobby didn't say anything except that he'd be gone a few days, but he'd be back. They drove off in Nobby's car, off towards Tug's place. And that's all I know, honestly.'

Ray Doyle sensed they were onto a loser with the girl. Bodie was crouched, peering into the cluttered shelves of a sideboard. Noticing the silence, he glanced back over his shoulder, and frowned. 'You don't mind, I hope . . . looking around . . .'

Doreen shook her head. Some inner train of thought was depressing her, because she suddenly seemed close to tears.

'It's all that Colonel's fault. He had a kind of power over Nobby, from the moment he arrived.'

Doyle tried to act sympathetically. 'How did he arrive?'

'On foot,' said Doreen. 'He was a right mess. I had to clean the mud off his clothes.'

'How did they get mud on them?' asked Bodie, reaching into the sideboard, and adding, not connected with his idle question, 'It's hollow back here.'

Doyle watched him from the sofa. Doreen was saying, 'How do you think? From all that walking . . .'

'All that walking?'

'The walking he took to get here. Nobby said it took him two days. In a straight line, by compass.' Doyle was surprised, and stared at the girl.

'He *walked* here?'

That was astonishing. Hembury Military Hospital was sixty miles away, as the crow flew. Sixty miles across country, in a straight line. That was dedication! What on earth drove a man to pack his case, quit a hospital, and trudge for two days, under cover, to a tiny, backwoods village, an old soldier, too trigger happy for his own good, all to do a pathetic bank job a hundred miles away? A robbery for less cash than he probably had in his current account?

Doreen added, almost tearfully. 'We had a good little place here. I know I moan a lot, but Nobby was good to me, and we'd have got a place closer to London eventually. And then he had to come, that crazy man. And he spoilt it!'

Bodie fell over backwards, and yelled with triumph. He was holding a piece of wood in his hands, having been required to exert some brute force on the hidden compartment, but now he could pull the side-board away from the wall.

Doyle and Doreen crossed the room and peered at the narrow, but wide, cache that had been hollowed out of the plaster.

Wrapped in oilskins, and tied with string, were nearly twenty different weapons.

'Look at this,' said Bodie fondly, pulling a Swedish Carl Gustav out of its protective skins. It was a beautiful weapon, and well cared for. 'Nine millimetre,' said Bodie, 'Fifty rounds. Used to use one of these with a silencer. Beautiful weapon.' He passed the automatic to Doyle, who hefted it appreciatively, and watched as Bodie unwrapped others. 'AK 47, Stirlings, and he's had a long weapon in here ...'

'The FN automatic,' said Doyle. 'They had one on the raid ...'

'I'd have used the Stirling,' said Bodie. 'Or taken another of these ...' and he held up a wicked looking shotgun, the barrel cut through fifteen inches from the chamber.

'Quite a little arsenal,' said Doyle.

'Oh my God,' said Doreen, in a voice trembling with anxiety. She stared at the cache and began to shake.

Perhaps she knew it was the end for Nobby Clarke.

Some little time after evening mess, an army jeep approached the gate-house of the Regimental Barracks at Offenden. It was a still, pleasant dusk, and the barracks were essentially in silence. The guards at the gate-house watched the approaching jeep, and stepped out to meet it as it pulled to a halt.

The driver was a small, stocky man, and his main passenger was a stern looking Lieutenant-Colonel, who seemed impatient with the essential check. They were all dressed in combat fatigues. In the back sat a corporal, holding on to two automatic rifles, and taking very little interest in anything.

'Just taking a break from Blue Zone training. Wanted to see Lieutenant-Colonel Manning. Any chance?'

The guard was taken aback. He would have expected some ID to be proferred, but he put two and two together and assumed that on Blue Zone training - whatever that was - one didn't carry such a thing.

'Who shall I say, sir?'

'Lieutenant-Colonel Peter Lawson. He'll know me.'

As the guard turned back to the small gatehouse, Lawson stepped from the jeep and stretched, walked round to stand close to the young soldier as he telephoned through to the barracks.

'This is the gatehouse, sir. Lieutenant-Colonel Peter Lawson to see you. Can I let him through?'

The young soldier listened for a moment, then passed the

phone to Lawson, who took it and heard Manning's cheery tones from the other end. 'Tony! Hello old boy!' he said.

'What the devil are you doing here, Peter . . .?' Manning asked.

'Got a brace of grouse for you, old chap; passing by, thought I'd drop them off!'

Manning was delighted. 'Come right up. You know where I'm billetted, I expect.'

'Of course.'

He handed the phone back to the guard, who listened, nodded, then acknowledged Manning's order. Lawson strolled jauntily back to the jeep and swung into it. The guard raised the barrier, and Nobby Clarke swung the vehicle through into the military grounds.

Lawson directed the way through the rows of huts, to the small compound where the ugly, Victorian buildings that were the camp's HQ were situated. As they sat in the jeep for a moment, Lawson silently pointed out the quarter-masters stores, about a hundred yards away.

'So far, so easy, eh men?'

'For a chap like you, sir,' said Nobby. 'If you're an officer, and you speak like a gentleman, you can get away with most things it seems to me.'

'You know what to do,' said Lawson, as he climbed from the jeep. 'Don't arouse suspicions. Remember, you have every right to be here.'

With a wink at Tug, Colonel Lawson walked up the steps and into the dark buildings that was the officers' living quarters. His arrival had been announced to the armed man who sat just inside the door, and Lawson advanced across the plushly carpetted foyer without hesitating. As he passed the desk the man who sat there said, 'Colonel Manning's quarters are on the first floor, sir.'

Lawson trotted easily up the marble staircase. Good God, he thought, this isn't so much an army base as a four star hotel.

Tony Manning was the same age as Lawson, but he looked after himself only half-heartedly and in consequence showed his age more. He was a chunky little officer, rather fat in the face, lined around the eyes, and with the mannerisms of a man who has enjoyed a few too many gin and tonics. He was dressed casually as he greeted Lawson, pummelling him on the arms, and shaking his hand vigorously.

'Peter old chap! What a very pleasant surprise. Thought you were on the Rhine.'

'I am,' said Lawson mysteriously. 'Blue Zone training . . .'

Manning looked blank for just a second, then nodded understandingly. 'Got you,' he said. 'Sounds like a tough do. Eh?'

'Doddle, actually. Good to be back in the old country, even if under these circumstances.'

'Quite so,' enthused Manning, and led Lawson into the room. 'I was just trying to decide whether or not to have another nightcap. What'll you have? Brandy? Scotch? Got a rather splendid Armagnac too, if you'd care for it.' He looked up from the drinks table, queryingly. 'Can drink, I suppose. On this, I mean on Blue Zone training.'

'Thank God yes,' said Lawson, amused at Manning's posture of understanding. 'And I'll have a large scotch, thanks.'

As Manning turned back to the tray of bottles, sorting among them for an appropriately old scotch, Lawson looked quickly around the room, listened to the corridor outside for a fleeting second, then stepped towards his old friend.

Manning was still prattling on. 'Now tell me . . .' he poured drink as he spoke. 'Just between the two of us – what is this bit of juice on the grapevine about you, eh? Knew it was all damned lies. Mess gossip . . .'

As he turned with the glass of whiskey in his hand, Lawson hit him ferociously on the side of the head with a cosh. Manning flew across the room, the glass dropping from his hand at the last minute and smashing against the wall. His body was sprawled across an armchair, but began to twist round, as if the unconscious man were trying to rise to his feet, but failed. Glassy eyed, bleeding from a split lip, Colonel Manning stayed put on the floor as Lawson walked to the drinks tray and swigged twelve year old scotch from the bottle.

By the following morning, the peaceful atmosphere of the barracks had been banished totally. The small parade ground was like a circus, with vans and cars of different hues – police, fire department, MI5 and of course CI5 – and a throng of people, all busily questioning and noting and preparing to make reports.

Most of the activity was centred around the weapons store, whose door now hung loosely by one hinge, and the ammunition building close by.

As George Cowley arrived in his own car, screeching to a halt at the edge of the parade ground, Bodie and Ray Doyle were busy questioning the guards who had been on duty the evening before. Both agents acknowledged their chief as he swept past, and then walked across to his car. Brigadier Tennant emerged from the ammunition building, looking grim faced and officious, scowling at Cowley as he approached, but saying nothing for the moment. He was accompanied by a pasty faced youth, in army rig, who was putting the finishing touches to a list. This was the quartermaster himself, and when he had finished writing he passed the clipboard to his angry Brigadier, who snatched it away from him almost impetuously.

At Cowley's car, the small group of ministry men gathered in silence.

'Tell us the worst,' said George Cowley, and Tennant read from the clip board.

'Twenty pounds of plastic explosive. Two boxes of detonators. Four cases of hand grenades. Two cases of stun grenades. Six cases of 7.6 millimetre rounds . . .'

'For their automatics,' said Doyle knowledgeably, and earned a scowl from the Brigadier.

'Two cases nine millimetre. One case Moroc smoke bombs. One dozen mortar bombs . . .' he flipped over the sheet, took a deep breath and went on. 'Three armalite rifles. Three infra red telescopic image detectors. Three machine pistols . . . one mortar.'

He looked up and around the group. 'Any comments?'

Bodie said, 'They knew what they were after.'

Doyle added. 'So they know what they're doing.'

Tennant said nothing, and Cowley asked, 'How is Colonel Manning?'

'I just spoke to the hospital. A severe fracture to the right temple. Emergency operation to remove a blood clot. He's unconscious now, but before he went down he didn't remember much. Enough to identify Lawson, however. Damn shame!'

George Cowley didn't respond, but looked around the barracks ground before asking, 'Which way did they head when they left?'

Ray Doyle said, 'North east.'

Bodie contributed, 'Police got one sighting about twenty miles from Thornton Heath, apparently still heading north. Since then, nothing. Vanished off the roads again.'

Cowley stared hard at his agents. 'What's the man up to? What's his plan? No ideas at all? The girl ...?'

Ray Doyle shrugged, hands in his pockets. 'Not much help. Except for the arms cache. Nobby Clarke was what you might call "a collector".'

'Army surplus ...' said Bodie with a smirk.

'Early retirement for a handful of weapons, stirlings, AK 47s, FNs ... We saw those in use ... Perhaps those rifles, the armalites they've just ripped off, mean recruitment. More men.'

Cowley winced. 'God, I hope not.'

Brigadier Tennant said, 'They've got enough equipment, then, to rob a few more local banks. Enough to equip a small army.'

But Cowley wasn't so sure. He could smell something bigger than a rat, and bigger than small-time bank robbery. He'd already decided that the robbery was a funding expedition, for equipment and supplies to stock a camp, hidden somewhere in the home counties, or the midlands. Lawson wouldn't have used his own money ... Too easy to draw attention to himself, too easy for his name to have been on a bank roster, ready for his arrival.

Lawson was thinking hard, that much was clear. And he was laughing at danger.

'Whatever game he's after,' George Cowley said in a whisper, 'It's bigger than a bank. And it's bigger than conventional weapons ... They could have taken a lot more from these stores.'

Brigadier Tennant looked momentarily grief stricken, then he pulled himself together, slapped the quartermaster's list back at the store-keeper, and said, 'I was afraid of that.'

Chapter Six

To the casual observer, Marston Dale looked little different from any other government research installation. The woodland around it had been cleared to a depth of two hundred yards. The compound was protected by two layers of high, electrified fencing, and dogs prowled between these two barriers. The single entranceway was guarded by two blocks of buildings, each with a man-strength of six. There was not one but two gate-barriers to pass.

All of this to stop admittance to what looked to be a most uninteresting cluster of white-washed three-storey buildings, and a row of grey sheds. Two cooling towers were an unusual addition at the far side of the installation, where some low, red brick structures gave the appearance of a hospital incinerator.

Beyond the research buildings, more wire, and then an expanse of Wiltshire countryside that was joyous to behold. Unbroken by house or road, the landscape of rolling hills, fields, and dense woodland looked as natural as any land could look in England in this latter part of the twentieth century.

Lawson beheld it joyously, drinking in the peaceful country through his high-powered binoculars. He lay flat on his stomach, on high ground above Marston Dale, and thought to himself that it was just such unspoiled countryside as this that he was acting for. To protect and preserve a spirit of England that was present in its people and in its landscape, but more and more threatened by the sickness that was apathy, and individuality, and promiscuity and worst of all, a decay of patriotic fervour.

He brought his magnified view back to the research establishment itself. He could see cars, and a few white coated technicians going about their business. MPs and other security agents strolled nonchalantly about the grounds, and lounged at their posts.

Disgraceful, thought Lawson. Such casualness in so important a research site.

Marston Dale was not just any old government centre. It was a military installation that both Ministry and Government preferred not to talk about too loudly. For what Marston Dale specialised in was the most inhumane of weapons.

Nerve gas.

Lawson had seen all he needed to see. He slipped back into cover, stood, and brushed the grass and dirt off his combat gear. Humming the National Anthem to himself, he walked briskly back through the woods, skirting trackways, and the main road that led to Marston Dale, until half an hour later he arrived at the small clearing that he had made his base.

The camp was well disguised, as had all their camps been. The jeep was covered with netting, garnished with leaves and twigs snapped from the surrounding trees. Patrols might go into the woods during the day, but they wouldn't come this far in. Even if they did, Lawson was satisfied that they'd walk right through the clearing and not notice the camouflaged equipment that was stored there.

Tug was cleaning a rifle, working a stiff mechanism with incongrous delicacy. Nobby was checking over the mortar, one of the last checks of the purloined equipment before they would be ready to move.

Lawson was well satisfied.

He ate a quick meal, and drank a cup of strong tea. Then he called his little army to him, set up a piece of flat wood against a tree trunk, to use as a blackboard, and quickly sketched some diagrams upon it.

He waved Nobby and Tug to sitting positions so that he could tower above them as he addressed them:

'My men . . . we are now poised for the final thrust of the three stage engagement known as Operation Britannica. If this last, and crucial, attack is successful, as I am confident it will be, we shall then be in a position to deliver an ultimatum to the enemy with terms which he will have no alternative but to accept.'

He paused, looked down at the featureless expressions on his men's faces, and smiled. 'Included in those terms, of course, will be remuneration and compensation for our troops. And, of course, a total absolvement of responsibility from all military actions that have occurred. The bank, Nobby. No one will bother you about that.'

Nobby Clarke liked the sound of that. Tug liked the sound of 'remuneration.' That meant money, didn't it? He was already richer than his wildest dreams, on his share of the bank job surplus. But there could never be enough 'remuneration' as far as he was concerned.

Lawson continued, his baton below his arm, his stance and aspect that of an American General. 'Before we go over the details one last time, let me remind you of the one fact that pervades and overrides every stage of the engagement. We are in possession of the eternal military advantage of surprise.' He hesitated, regarded his two men, then peered intensely into the distance. 'And let us never forget that God, if he is an Englishman, is almost certainly on our side . . .'

In the planning room at Offenden Military HQ, a large map of Southern England had been spread out across the vast, oakwood table. Using a pointer, Brigadier Tennant was pointing out military installations in the area, and the location of key sites in connection with Peter Lawson and his private army.

Sipping tea, George Cowley surveyed the map with an expert eye, getting a feeling of the countryside in his mind, reconstructing hills and landscapes from the confusion of contours before him. Ray Doyle was leaning on the table, doing something very similar. Bodie stood with his arms folded, looking almost bored as he went though Lawson's known actions in his own mind.

Brigadier Tennant was still being subject to questions shot at him by the abrasive young men of CI5. He wasn't used to such gruff treatment, and half wished the men were in some way under his control, so that he could snap them into silence occasionally. But CI5 was a unit unto itself, hard men with a hard job to do, and often a hard, no-nonsense way of going about that job.

The phone rang and Cowley answered it, placing his mug down on the table and turning away from the map.

Tennant thought it might have been for him, and waited, expectantly, but Cowley kept talking into the receiver and didn't turn back.

Ray Doyle suddenly straightened and shot a question at the Brigadier. 'Listen, that army manoeuvre of Lawson's which went wrong in Germany. Come on, what *precisely* went wrong?'

'I'm not in a position . . .' began Brigadier Tennant, and straightened in irritation as Bodie cut in abusively, 'Never mind your positions, Brigadier. What happened?'

Cowley glanced round, on the phone, but said nothing, Tennant flustered for a moment, then shook his head, trying to out-stare Doyle and failing.

'I told you. His battalion was wiped out. He then turned on his own HQ . . .'

George Cowley had replaced the phone and now faced the other three, surveying them with that cool, Scottish thoughtfulness. 'All power stations, nuclear stations and major security installations have been alerted. If Lawson tries anything, he'll not know what hit him.'

Tennant picked up on this, as a welcome way of escaping the aggressive young men beside him. 'Hope it doesn't come to that, George . . .'

Again Ray Doyle cut in. Sharply, a man whose own life might soon be on the line, Doyle was in no mood for any more bushbeating; he snapped, 'Not good enough, Brigadier. How exactly *was* his battalion wiped out?'

Bodie said, cynically, 'From his expression it must have been a local cruise missile.'

Tennant gave Bodie a withering look, then turned his flushed face on Cowley. Cowley shook his head. 'You'll have to tell us, Bill. We'll have to know . . .'

Tennant gave in, shaking his head, moaning quietly. 'My God. I'd hoped it would never have to come out . . .' he looked up, straightened up, smoothed his moustaches and took a deep breath. 'Not a cruise missile, Mister Bodie. Something far worse . . . gas. Something to be ashamed of. Something appalling.'

Cowley caught his own breath sharply. He at last understood why Tennant had been so distraught about the action of his best friend's son.

But there was no time for sympathy now. Lawson was deadly dangerous. 'What sort of gas?' he prompted, and Tennant said, 'I'm quite sure that by telling you this I'm breaching every law of security there is. The gas was C29. Having told you that I might as well resign right now . . . if it ever gets further than the three of you.'

He looked around pointedly at the hard faces of CI5.

George Cowley glanced at his two men, and spoke for them all. 'It gets no further than this table, Bill. C29,' he repeated. 'That's a nerve gas, I imagine.'

'Yes. Deadly.'

'I thought we'd renounced the use of that particular weapon. I thought nerve gas was outlawed, now, by agreement with both sides.'

'We have to know how to defend ouselves against it,' said Tennant, running a shaking hand through his hair. 'You can't just ignore a weapon, no matter how filthy that weapon might be.'

Ray Doyle grasped, now, what had happened in Germany. 'Then one side, during that exercise, might have been using, or pretending to use, C29, a nerve gas . . . gas war practice . . .'

Cynically, Bodie put in, 'Practising for those times when we won't use it, of course . . .'

George Cowley banged his finger on the table, speculating wildly. 'Using a gas in a practice situation . . . a situation that Lawson objected to. Would I be right in that, Bill? Was he opposed to any use of gas at all?'

Brigadier Tennant didn't know the answer to that. 'We're all opposed, George. Lawson might have been a little more fanatical about it than the rest of us . . .'

'You mean the profile never indicated such a thing,' said Ray Doyle. 'Or he was never asked . . .'

Bodie said, 'This C29 gas . . . If we *did* have any, where would we . . . Where would it be stocked?'

Tennant said. 'It's kept where it's made. It's still under test, still too unpredictable for it to be dispatched ready for an contingency requiring active utilisation . . .'

'Where's it made?' asked Doyle, cutting through the jargon.

Tennant glanced at Cowley, hoping for some support,

some sign that the questioning would stop. But Cowley just stared at him, and Tennant conceded, 'At a place called Marston Dale.'

Both Bodie and Doyle leapt for the map, turning it slightly and running their fingers across the landmarks. 'We're here,' said Doyle, 'And where was that jeep sighted?'

Bodie stabbed a finger down, tapping the spot. Doyle picked up a metal ruler, laid it between the two points, slashed an ink marker along the edge. He moved the ruler to continue the line, and the edge coincided more or less with the location of Marston Dale.

'Straight lines,' said Bodie. 'Always in straight lines.'

'Marston Dale,' said Cowley. 'Bill, get in touch with them immediately. Warn them. It's a long shot . . .'

Bodie cut in, 'But it's all we've got!'

At exactly 2 pm Nobby cut the telephone lines to Marston Dale. It was an operation accomplished quickly and efficiently, and although there was a risk that the action would draw attention to the phones, Lawson was prepared to gamble that risk against the greater convenience of having the installation's communications in a jam.

He spoke quickly, bluntly into the R/T. 'Lines cut. Proceeding to Synchronisation Point A. Out.'

Tug's voice was a grim, brief acknowledgement at the other end of the channel.

'Ready Sergeant?'

'Ready, sir,' said Nobby Clarke, and followed Lawson to the jeep. He glanced back and up the slopes behind the Dale, to where he imagined he could see Tug Willis, watching them, one hand on the mortar for luck, no doubt.

Nobby revved up the jeep, and swung in out of concealment and onto the road that led to the gatehouse of Marston Dale. They said nothing as they drove, and Nobby felt a tight knot of tension in his stomach. But when he glanced at Lawson he saw that the Colonel was half smiling, totally relaxed. Enjoying the action.

At the entrance to the government station Nobby jammed on the brakes. Two uniformed security men ran towards the vehicle, swinging high powered automatic rifles into service. Lawson jumped down to the road and calmly, but hurriedly, approached the men, his hands away from his body. Behind the two guards he could see two other security men training rifles on him.

'Colonel Walters! Bomb disposal!' he shouted. 'Don't hesitate man, get on the blower to admin. Tell them I'm here . . .'

One man hesitated, then turned and raced back to the gatehouse. The other guard looked uncertainly at Lawson, and lowered his rifle. Nobby Clarke drove the jeep forward slightly, pressing the accelerator in bursts to give a sound as of emergency.

'What's going on, sir?' asked the guard.

Lawson wiped a hand across his brow, glanced at his watch with apprehension; the guard would have heard his muttered statement of 'My God, it's nearly time . . .'

Aloud he said, 'We have reports that an IRA bomb has been placed here. Marston Dale is a designated target . . . Where *is* the entry order. For God's sake, man . . .'

A senior guard came out of the hut. 'We had an alert a few minutes ago, but no one said what it was about . . . phones are down. There's no one responding at admin . . .'

Again Lawson checked his watch. 'Get somebody quick, *quick* . . .' he snapped at the young guard in front of him, and the man turned an ran towards the distant buildings. The corporal came quickly towards Lawson, his face a mask of confusion and uncertainty. 'I'll ride with you,' he said. 'It should be all right!'

All further decisions were made easier a moment later.

Up on the hill Tug had been watching the gatehouse confrontation. The second time Lawson had looked at his watch Tug had loaded a mortar shell into the stolen weapon, ducked away, and listened to the dull thud as the shell was fired.

It hit the compound beyond the first line of buildings, with an immense explosion, a great crashing of glass and a pall of black smoke that coursed swiftly up into the air.

That was too much for the gate-guards. Lawson immediately assumed control 'Quick man, the place must be evacuated! Ring the alarm, then ride with me . . .'

He turned and ran to the the jeep. Nobby revved the engine and ran at the barrier. The corporal, almost without thought, turned and raised the barrier, shouted 'Raise the alarm. The alarm!' and jumped onto the back of the vehicle.

'Where's the P.A. Control?' shouted Lawson as they sped into the compound. The guard, hanging onto the back of Tug's jeep for all he was worth, tried to stab a finger in the general direction. People were pouring out of buildings, now, and a siren had started to *whoop*.

Tug, up on the hill, was following orders precisely, and another explosion sounded distantly, allowing Lawson a cry of 'My God, there's more than one. I knew as much . . .'

At the P.A. room Lawson slapped Nobby's shoulder and the jeep screeched to a halt, precipitating the guard into the back seat. As he struggled upright again Lawson ran into the small building, taking out a hand grenade and removing the pin.

'Mind out!' he shouted. 'There's a bomb somewhere in the room!' He spotted the short wave transmitter, and stood firm as the rooms three occupants fled through the door. Then he tossed the grenade into the equipment and backed out as a deafening blast knocked him to the ground, and sent a spray of plaster and wire fragments into the corridor.

He had no need to urge panic now. The whole installation must have been on its toes.

The guard had vanished from the jeep by the time Lawson was outside. Nobby jerked his head backwards, and indicated that it was safe. 'Right,' said Lawson calmly. 'Get a smoke bomb ready.'

He could see the distant flash on the hill of the mortar. He hoped nobody else would notice.

They drove slowly through the throngs of people, and the confusion. 'Are they bombs, or is someone shooting at us?' he heard someone say, and had the presence of mind to shout, 'Whole installation's been rigged. Get into the open!'

Nobby drove on, following Lawson's directions. They came to a dull looking building, not many windows, not many entrances. 'That's it,' said Lawson. 'Use the smoke.'

Nobby looked about cautiously, then chucked the smoke canister some yards away. Billowing clouds of white smoke rapidly engulfed the buildings around.

'You know what to look for . . .' he said, and Nobby affirmed.

Holding their FN automatics in classic troop style, barrel downwards but ready for instant action in any direction, they trotted into the building. Smash a window or two, let the smoke in,' said Lawson, and Nobby duly obliged. Now as they moved through the corridors, smoke followed them.

In their camouflage, combat outfits, faces blackened, eyes alight with tension, they looked too officious to argue with, and as white-coated staff met them in the corridor those same staff, whether junior or senior, responded instantly to Lawson's snapped command to 'GET OUT OF THE BUILDING!'

A mortar exploded close by.

'Damn,' said Lawson, hearing the thump and rattle of glass through the shouts and cries of the panicking staff. 'I told him to steer well clear of this spot.' Another explosion, this time showering glass into the building just ahead of the two of them as they moved swiftly towards the target room.

A second siren started to whine, and a bell rang, perhaps a fire bell.

But at last Lawson had found the room he wanted, a heavily locked door marked with the skull symbol of warning, and the added declaration KEEP OUT.

'Blast it,' he said to Nobby, and the smaller man dropped his rifle, crouched by the door and expertly applied plastic explosive to the stress points.

He ran a wire a few yards back, niftily attached the ends to a small detonator, and blasted the door open with a billow of smoke, but hardly any sound.

'Follow me,' snapped Lawson, and burst through the choking result of the explosion, into the errily tranquil room, where a single orange light illuminated rows of shelves. The shelves were stacked with cannisters, all of them dull and grey, all labelled with nothing but numbers.

Swiftly Lawson walked down the aisles seeking the cannisters he wanted. Nobby found them first, and Lawson hurried over.

'Take two,' said Lawson, and as Nobby loaded up a haversack, Lawson himself hefted the cannister he had picked up, stroking the cold metal surface, almost lovingly caressing the simple code:

C29.

When Nobby had loaded the gas, and secured the haversack, he picked up his rifle again. Lawson slapped him on the shoulder and grinned. 'Good work, excellent work. Now let's get the hell out of here.'

Glowing with pride Nobby began the long run back through the system of corridors that led to the outside. He preceded Lawson, who ran cautiously in the rear.

It had indeed been a dangerous mission, but Nobby felt a great swelling pride in his chest as he thought of how they had almost pulled it off. Wouldn't Tug be envious, stuck up there on the hill, letting off mortar fire but not really in the heat of the action. Maybe there'd even be a medal in it for him. After all, this was an undercover operation, and even if it wasn't totally official, the secret services had ways of quietly honouring those who had served them well.

He was still running through this fantasy in his mind when he reached the door, pushed through it into the smokey day. He ran across to the jeep, turning to watch for Lawson. He dumped the haversack into the back seats, and laid his FN automatic carefully on top. Lawson staggered through the door of the research building, and stumbled.

Nobby started to go and help the Colonel.

But the blast of a mortar lifted him upwards and backwards, flung him broken and bloody across the jeep and to the rough ground beyond.

Lawson reached the vehicle and dumped his own rifle. He ran round to Nobby's crumpled corpse and dragged it to the jeep, heaving it into the passenger seat. Three men were running towards him, white coated, young, probably technicians.

He had to think fast again. 'Get down!' he yelled. 'Lie flat . . . for God's sake, get down!'

As the three men flung themselves to the ground and covered their heads, Lawson tossed a grenade back to the door of the building, then climbed into the driver's seat of the jeep and sped away to the main gate.

Within seconds he had passed the empty gate-house, left the billowing smoke behind, and was speeding along the road to the rendezvous point with Tug.

Bodie's face was calm with concentration as he sped the Capri along the winding, country road that led to Marston Dale. He had been driving for over twenty minutes without speaking, without hesitation, his right foot practically motionless on the accelerator.

Beside him, being thrown to right and left as the car swerved and dodged around the slow moving traffic of the countryside, Ray Doyle had checked his heavy magnum, snatched two glucose tablets to help keep his mind alert, and now frantically spoke to CI5 control.

'4.5 here. Have you got through to that number yet?'

He didn't like what Control had to report. 'Negative. Trouble with the line.'

'Short wave contact?'

'Negative, 4.5. Oh, message from Alpha one. Your contact at Marston Dale is Professor Kaveney.'

'Copy, control. 4.5 out.'

Doyle rested the R/T in his lap, stared grimly ahead at the curving road and the flashing kerbside trees and hedges. 'Can't you go any faster?' he said to Bodie, as a Ford Cortina swerved to avoid the racing Capri.

Within minutes they had passed over the ridge that led down to Marston Dale.

'My God . . .!' was Doyle's only comment as he and Bodie got the first inkling of trouble.

A great pall of grey smoke rose above the landscape, rising from the exact position of the government station. Neither CI5 man said another word - there was nothing useful to say at this precise moment - and Doyle hung on to his seat-belt as Bodie proved that the Capri was well able to travel at close to one hundred mph across a field.

They bumped and lurched onto the road a half mile distant, screeched through ninety degrees, and approached the gate house of Marston Dale as if they were at Brands Hatch. Armed men stood there in a solid line, heavy armalite rifles pointed menacingly at the approaching car. There would be no further mistakes.

Doyle had his and Bodie's ID ready, and he didn't make the mistake of being too pushy. The soldier who inspected the cards, and the two men, was hard-faced and looked for all the world as if he'd as soon shoot them as risk a second duping.

At last he called for one of the security men. 'Ride with them. First sign of tricks, blow their frigging heads off.'

'Sir!' snapped the soldier, and climbed into the back seats of the Capri, resting his pistol easily on his lap.

The barrier was lifted. Bodie drove on through.

'What happened?' Doyle asked their uninvited passanger.

'About ten bombs detonated,' said the soldier. 'All over the centre. More fire than bomb damage. Bombs quite small ... Someone thinks they might even have been mortars, but there was so much smoke.'

'Any dead?' asked Bodie, and the soldier grunted. 'Too many. And one of *them*, we reckon. They got away, but one of them looked none too well in the front seat.'

Doyle and Bodie jumped from the car as they arrived at the great gathering of technicians, police, army and scientists. All around them the research unit was in ruins, blasted buildings, fire-gutted sheds, but now most of the fire was out, and the concrete walk-ways were slick with water and foam.

Doyle located Professor Kaveney, a middle aged man, tall, thin and greying, his face rimmed, now, with smoke grime, his eyes wild and concerned as he tried to comprehend exactly what had happened.

The CI5 men had put no more than two questions to him when Kaveney was called urgently from the main building. The three of them ran to the three-storey centre, where most of the laboratories were located, and paced down the corridor to the security room where, with a gasp of horror, Professor Kaveney saw for the first time the door, blasted off its hinges.

They stepped inside. Kaveney walked slowly through the racks of cannisters, Bodie and Doyle tentatively following, watching, waiting.

'Anything missing?' prompted Doyle, and Kaveney said, 'I don't think there is. Must have been after money ...' And then he saw what had been stolen, and gasped.

'Oh my God no ... Not that ...'

Doyle hurried after him. 'What'd they get?'

'They couldn't have taken anything worse . . .' Kaveney's face had taken on a haunted, terrified look. 'They must have known exactly what they were after.'

'C29,' said Bodie dully.

'C29,' agreed the Professor. 'The most toxic substance on the planet.'

They had buried Nobby in a shallow grave, and Lawson had spoken consoling words while Tug had stood looking mournful, guilty, and ultimately devastated.

'It was my fault,' he said grimly, his big frame shaking.

'Nonsense, Corporal,' said Lawson. 'Pull yourself together man.'

'If I hadn't fired that last bomb he would still be alive.'

'You were both obeying orders, Tug. He knew the risks.'

'Yeah, but . . .'

Lawson cut in sharply, yet with a touch of humanity in his voice. 'Chin up, Tug. Don't worry. Nobby's death will not have been in vain.' He strode to the jeep and picked up two cannisters of C29, waved them at Tug. 'I promise you that.'

Chapter Seven

The control room of CI5 buzzed with activity as the full ramifications of Lawson's action at Marston Dale began to come clear. Telephones shrilled, monitors, flickered, uniformed men carried sheafs of flimsys between one station and the next.

Ray Doyle was tired, but alert, standing quietly by the stiff, concerned shape of Professor Kaveney, who nibbled on his nails as he waited for George Cowley to finish with a phone call. Bodie, hands hooked into his belt, lounged against a filing cabinet, running the events of the previous few hours through his mind.

Cowley was saying, 'The jeep was found on the motorway, yes. That's right. We make the assumption they were heading for London . . . That's right, operations centre is now back here . . . Yes sir. Yes, will do.'

He placed the red phone down, loosened his tie and drew it off, unbuttoning the top of his shirt. It was indeed getting hot in the control room.

'The Minister has been informed,' he said, more to Bodie and Doyle than any others. 'He's in Cabinet conference, and will advise the P.M. as and when necessary.' He turned back to Kaveney, who had seemed to shrink inside his baggy grey suit. 'Continue please, Professor.'

Kaveney shrugged his broad, hollow shoulders. His grey eyes flickered restlessly over the three men beside him. 'As I said, they've taken two cannisters, each one containing three litres of liquefied C29 gas.'

'Don't the cannisters require refrigeration?' asked Cowley, and Kaveney shook his head.

'No, no. They're in pressurised vacuum.'

'And when the contents are released?'

Kaveney drew in a breath, stared at the ground ahead of him, as if uncomfortable with meeting the solemn, searching stares of the young agents. 'The liquid . . . Boils. It rapidly becomes gas under normal atmospheric conditions.'

'And then?' asked Ray Doyle quietly.

'It disperses ... Extremely quickly.'

'How quickly?' asked George Cowley, watching the scientist through narrowed, hostile eyes.

'Well, it could cover several square miles within minutes. It depends, of course, on wind strength. In strong winds it will spread across that area in, well, seconds.'

Ray Doyle and Bodie exchanged an impassive but telling look. Neither of them had any time for gas, both having run up against gases of one sort or another during their wildly different careers, prior to becoming agents of CI5. Doyle asked, 'And just how toxic is it?'

'I'm afraid the answer to that is not good news. Just one part in a million can be lethal.'

'Good God,' said Cowley, appalled, and shared Doyle's look of horror.

Doyle asked, 'You mean, then, that everyone within miles of an exploded cannister would die within seconds if they took a breath of air ...'

'It doesn't have to be breathed,' said Kaveney. 'This is the whole point of C29 as a gas deterrent ... The molecules, on contact with animal tissue, that could be skin, lungs, they produce a chain reaction within the nervous system. Once that happens, death occurs in a very short space of time ...'

'Just a touch to the skin,' echoed Bodie, shaking his head. He had never come up against anything like this, nothing either so deadly or so terrifying in its action. Gases to make you laugh helplessly, or lose control of your innards, or blind you, choke you, put you to sleep ... But he'd always felt he could outrun a gas. He was an athlete, he could sprint longer than most men could jog. But a gas that touched one tiny bit of the skin of your neck, and could still kill ...

He asked, 'It can spread in seconds, you say. OK. How wide an area could it expand to and still remain deadly?'

Kaveney thought for a quick moment, then rubbed his hand across the back of his neck. 'Well, it's molecular weight is about the same as that of air. When the atmospheric pressure is heavy, like today, it would spread farther in a sideways direction. The actual *weight* of air above it would keep if from dissipating upwards.'

'So the maximum lethal area would be . . .?' prompted Bodie, who didn't really want to hear the answer. Ray Doyle shuffled restlessly beside him, staring at the Professor in an almost truculant way.

Kaveney drew out a pocket calculator, stabbed at it a few times, then shrugged. 'I can't answer that question gentlemen. There are too many variables. It would certainly be in excess of twenty linear miles in the direction of the wind, in an arc with an angle not less than 45 degrees . . .'

Ray Doyle winced, looked hard at Cowley who had gone quite pale. 'And they've got *two* cannisters,' the younger man said.

'My God,' said George Cowley. 'I begin to get an idea of what Lawson's up to.'

Tug Willis had just finished taping a hand grenade to one of the C29 canisters when the coded knock at the rear doors of the Bedford Van preceded Lawson's entrance.

Tug's hand went to his automatic rifle, just in case, but only his Colonel stepped into the dark-windowed van, closing the doors behind him. 'Everything all right sir?' asked Tug.

'Everything's fine, Corporal,' said Lawson. 'Streets are quiet. A lot of police, as expected, but no sign of panic. They're not sure we're here yet.'

He placed a large paper package onto the small work-bench that Tug had set up, and unwrapped several wire contraptions that the soldier didn't recognise. Lawson merely smiled and said, 'You'll see.'

Outside a fire engine passed with a noisy wailing of its two tone siren. Tug watched it go, then looked back up the street, confident that no-one could see his thick set features peering out at him.

They were in South London. It was mid-afternoon and the activity of shoppers and school-children was quite heavy.

'How's the weather, Corporal?'

Tug glanced at the notes he had taken a few minutes before. 'Er, light winds, sir. And they're in the north-east.

Directly towards the West End from where we are.'

'Excellent. Atmospheric pressure?'

'One thousand and twenty eight millibars. Whatever that means.'

'What that means, Tug, is that everything is perfect. Let's have a look at the canister.'

Tug passed the C29 can, and its attached grenade, and Lawson hefted it in his hands. He grinned at Tug. 'Feels just about right. Now, where's that parcel you have to deliver?'

Tug picked up the heavy cardboard box that he'd already wrapped in brown paper, and addressed. There was a hand-written envelope taped to the outside of the box. Inside, Tug knew, lay the second canister of C29.

He laid the parcel down beside the grenade canister, and Lawson breathed deeply, satisfied that everything was working to plan.

'Excellent. Now, Tug. How do you feel? Quite confident?'

Tug shrugged. He still didn't have an inkling of what Colonel Lawson was up to, but at least his own part in the plan had been made clear to him. 'I feel fine sir,' he said. 'Just a little anxious, I suppose.'

'Don't worry. I know what's bothering you. We'll come to that now.'

He reached into his civilian coat pocket and drew out two thick manila envelopes. One was addressed to Nobby Clarke, the other to Tug himself.

'Listen carefully, Tug,' said the Colonel, and Tug leaned forward attentively. Lawson went on, 'As of the completion of your next job, you are finished with the mission, and free to return to your old way of life. These letters on behalf of you, and Nobby's next of kin – the girl Doreen – contain instructions to my bank in Geneva.' He handed the letters to Tug. 'You will each be paid one half of the balance of my numbered account, or one million pounds sterling, whichever is the greater. I've made all the appropriate arrangements. Nothing can go wrong.'

Tug hefted the envelopes. There was more than a letter in each of them.

Colonel Lawson went on, 'The account is quite healthy. There's a little something in there for temporary expenses.

Even if the final stage of our operation does not succeed, your cheque will still be very substantial. And as for the balance of the proceeds of our first requisition, well, that is yours as well, to be collected at your convenience from where we left it. Your envelope also contains a signed statement from me that at all times you acted under orders . . . My orders.'

'Thank you sir,' said Tug, overwhelmed by what he was hearing. But better was to come, for Lawson had stood as best he could in the cramped back of the van, beckoned Tug to his feet, and laid a hand on his shoulder.

'That letter also records your promotion, Willis, as of this moment to Colour Sergeant.'

Tug was speechless with delight. Colour Sergeant! It was a rank he had long since given up any hope of attaining.

'I don't know what to say, sir,' he finally managed to stutter.

'I understand, Tug. Say nothing. But let's check our watches!'

They synchronised time-pieces, and then came the final checks. 'You have it clear, now, Tug, exactly what you have to do?' Lawson fixed his man with an authoritative stare, and Tug straightened as best he could, and nodded. 'Yes sir.'

'You are completely confident?'

'I have confidence in you, sir. I'll carry out my part.'

'Then let us wish each other the best of luck.'

They shook hands, solemnly. Tug picked up the parcel and stepped from the van, closing the doors on Colonel Lawson, and on the final stage of Operation Britannica.

He waited a few minutes as per instructions, sitting on a park bench, his face hidden behind a copy of the *Guardian*. Few people were about, mostly older couples, walking a dog, or ambling slowly in the warm air. Children played noisily in the park, but they were not concerned with the fat man reading his paper.

Checking his watch repeatedly, Tug at last stood up and began to walk north, to the street that Lawson had decided in advance would be used for the contact. Tug was wearing a parka, and looked quite immense as he strolled along the pavement, looking for a likely 'target'. He carried the canister underneath his arm.

He saw a middle aged man stepping briskly towards him, and decided that this was the individual he would use. The man was dressed like a city gent, except that he wore no bowler hat. He looked pale faced and soft.

Tug grinned. Easy.

As the man passed, Tug stepped forward. 'Excuse me . . .'

The pedestrian stopped and smiled, but the smile was a nervous one as Tug stepped towards him. 'Yes?'

'Do me a favour,' said Tug Willis, and added more menacingly, 'Or I'll blow your head off . . .'

As he spoke he opened his parka coat slightly and allowed the man to see the butt of his machine pistol. The man's eyes widened with fear and surprise, and Tug stepped even closer, glancing about him to make sure that no-one was looking.

'I want you to take this parcel and give it to the first copper you see. I'll be following you, right?' The pedestrian nodded dumbly, his eyes still half on Tug's face, half on the gun. 'I'm a crack shot,' said Tug, 'And this gun has a long range. I'll have the back of your head off and be in Soho in the space of two seconds. So you do it right. Right?'

'Right,' said the man, and took the parcel from Tug's hands. He hurried away, not looking back, and Tug grinned and dodged back the way he had come, trotting down alleys, and side-streets until he was sure he had put half a mile between himself and the point of contact.

Then he drew a small R/T from his pocket, fiddled with it, called Lawson a couple of times, and at last picked up Lawson's rasped response.

'Patriot One to Patriot Leader. Message delivered. Over.'

'Patriot Leader. Good work. Out.'

Tug hid the R/T in the voluminous pockets of his parka and began to stroll nonchalantly to the nearest tube station.

When Tug had left the van, Lawson had moved up into the driver's seat and slowly driven the Bedford round the streets of this part of London until he had come to his own target point.

A large playground, tarmac covered for the most part, and quite crammed with exercise and games equipment. There were several children playing there, mostly on the slide. Distantly a few parents idled and talked, or sat on the grass watching their offspring kicking balls about. The park around the playground was quite densely covered with trees, and a few patches of bush and flower beds.

Lawson, wearing casual clothes, and a warm-wind-cheater, walked quickly to the swings, unconcerned by the curious glances of several of the small kids, who followed him as he walked, exchanging puzzled glances.

Lawson stopped at the swings and lowered his haversack to the ground. He reached up with a screwdriver and disconnected the middle swing from its hooks, throwing the apparatus some way away. 'Get out of here!' he shouted at the small group of gawping infants, and the four of them scattered at the gruff sound of his voice.

They continued to watch from a distance as Lawson tied two lengths of nylon wire to the crossbar of the swings. Then he reached back to the haversack and drew out a peculiar metal framework, onto which he attached several round car-mirrors. He tied the ends of the wire to the frame, shortened the wire, and appeared satisfied. Finally he fixed a small earpiece to his left ear, tuned his tiny radio transmitter correctly, and sat down below the cross-bar of the swings. The last item of apparatus he produced was a small, battery powered TV which he placed in front of him and began to watch.

All hell broke loose in CI5 at precisely 4.10 pm. Earlier, Cowley had co-ordinated the setting up of anti-nerve gas units at the four corners of Greater London. Every available man in CI5 was stationed on maximum alert about the capital, and the control room itself was now linked directly to the Prime Minsiter. There was little else that could have been done at that time, and Cowley and Professor Kaveney had spent a restless, nervous hour or so staring out across the city.

Wondering where Lawson would strike ... If indeed he planned to strike today at all!

But their alertness was repaid, their state of readiness not an unneccessary precaution. For contact was made, via Tug's terrified target pedestrian, at 4.09 pm. Within a minute Whitehall was practically totally mobilised. The streets of London screamed with the noise of bells and sirens, heading south. CI5 was stripped of waiting men, all but Cowley who remained on the phone, writing down in detail the several demands that Lawson had apparently made in his hand-written note.

Only when that was finished did he pick up his R/T and make contact with Bodie and Doyle. 'Sector Four,' he said, and gave the precise co-ordinates. 'As fast as you can.'

He turned to face Professor Kaveney, his lips pinched and white. His hands shook as he held up the piece of paper on which he had been scribbling the notes.

'Lawson's demands,' he explained.

'What are they?'

'He has given us one hour in which to blow up the entire chemical warfare research establishments at three separate locations . . .'

Kaveney was horrified, almost flabbergasted. 'He's mad. He's a madman!'

'He has the lives of millions in the palm of his left hand,' said Cowley. 'This operation has been planned to the last detail. Mad? Yes, perhaps. But brilliantly so. He wants the destruction of the three sites to be relayed by ENG TV on all channels, so he can see it happen . . . Live . . .'

'One hour. All that work, wasted . . . You're not going . . .'

Cowley cut him short with a sound that was part hostility, part impatience. 'He also wants two million pounds transferred to a Swiss account. And he wants the National Anthem played on Radio 2 . . .' Even Cowley could not hold back the glimmer of a smile as he relayed this, 'Every hour, on the hour . . . until the year two thousand and twenty!'

It was time. Lawson did not under-estimate the speed with which the British secret services would act, following Tug's contact. So it was time to get into position.

Zero hour.

Lawson rose to his feet, looking very weird indeed. He had removed his coat and had fastened the curious metal frame about his shoulders. The wing-mirrors were attached to this frame, pointing backwards, so that as he stood he could see the playground behind him.

He picked up the canister, with its attached grenade, then stood up on a small stool and tied the end of the nylon wire, dangling from the cross-frame of the swings, to the pin of the grenade. Carefully, then, he stepped down from the stool and kicked it away. His arm was fully outstretched, holding the canister of C29 above his head. He had no leeway. If he lowered his arm by even half an inch, the pin of the grenade would be yanked free.

And there would be four seconds to doomsday!

But he was well trained for this. At Hembury he had trained himself morning, noon and night. The muscles of his arms were taut, and immensely strong. His left arm was the strongest, and this is the arm that he had chosen to support the weight of the heavy canister.

He knew, from his own experience, that he could hold the canister above his head for up to an hour. Then the blood, draining from his arm, and the pure fatigue of motionlessness would cause the arm to drop . . .

The pin to pull . . .

The explosion to occur . . .

When he said there was an hour to accomplish his demands, he meant an hour exactly. He had not built flexibility into his plans.

He took a deep breath as the muscles of his body began to move and strain in their new posture. He heard the laughter of the children who were watching him, and he smiled at them. He could see others in the mirrors on his shoulders.

He waited.

And it wasn't long before the first screeching sound of brakes and tyres told him that the forces of law and order were moving in.

The police had cleared the park, using loudhailers, by the time Bodie and Doyle arrived at the scene. A cordon of police and army had been set up round the park, and the last curious onlookers were being hustled out through the main gates. The flashing blue of lights, on police cars, ambulances and fire-engines, seemed to cast an eerie atmosphere over the roadway outside. Inside: the single man, standing below the swing, his arm uplifted to heaven.

Bodie led the way into the park, to an observation point about a hundred yards from Lawson, screened by bushes and several immature trees. Using binoculars the two men scanned Lawson's features ...

'Looks tired,' said Bodie.

'Looks determined,' added Doyle.

Behind them, two strange shaped vans drove slowly into the park, and drew up close by. Several men wearing bizarre white suits leapt out of the backs, and deployed. The suits, Bodie knew, were anti-gas suits, thickly rubberised, totally sealed, with great flapping head-covers through which sound was always muffled. Line of sight was through square windows. Ability to move: not very much. The suits were cumbersome and heavy, and when the CI5 men were offered such protection, they refused.

Cowley arrived, with the Professor from Marston Dale. He and the police chief of greater London set up a bonnet HQ on Cowley's car, and talked urgently for a few moments, before Cowley walked across to Doyle. Bodie had slipped forward a little, but re-appeared from the bushes, passing his binoculars to Cowley.

'How do you read it?' asked the Scot quickly. He peered into the distance, adjusting the zoom facility of the binoculars.

Bodie said, matter-of-factly, 'The second he drops his arm that grenade will go off in four seconds.'

Ray Doyle was frantically trying to think of alternatives. He said, 'We could hit the wire with a high-powered bullet. But we couldn't guarantee a hit first time, and the shock wave, if it missed very narrowly, would pull the pin out.'

'Good thinking,' said Cowley, and lowered the binoculars. He looked at his two men, but was in fact deep in thought. 'How about a laser?'

Bodie shook his head. 'He'd see us setting it up and might act prematurely. Besides, we couldn't rig one up in time.'

'Four seconds ...' mused Cowley. 'And if we go closer than this ... A hundred yards, perhaps, he'll blow himself sky high. A hundred yards in four seconds ...'

'Not possible,' said Bodie. 'Not even for Superman.'

Cowley called Professor Kaveney over. 'Is there any chance that the canister could survive a close grenade explosion?'

Kaveney shrugged, stared cautiously out at Lawson. 'I just don't know. They're certainly designed to withstand a lot of external pressure, but an explosion at such close range? I'd have to test one …'

Ray Doyle shook his head, looked dismissive of the suggestion. 'You could test one in less than an hour? Properly test one?'

'I don't think so.'

And Bodie said. 'Who says we've got an hour? He may think he can hold it up that long, but what if he gets cramp? Uh-uh.' He shook his head, and smiled without humour. 'We've got to come up with something *now*,' and he took back his binoculars and turned to study Lawson again.

Cowley walked back to his car, where a knot of army and police exchanged ideas in heated fashion. The TV monitor had been set up here and Cowley stared at it for a moment, then reached for his R/T. 'Cowley. Are those ENG Units installed yet?'

The voice of a technician came back. 'About another ten minutes …'

Picking up a loudhailer, George Cowley returned to the edge of the arena, followed by the police chief. 'We've got nothing to lose by trying a few simple tricks …'

Raising the hailer to his lips he called, 'Colonel Peter Lawson. This is George Cowley of CI5. We are setting up ENG surveillance now at the establishments you requested! But the Government has not yet given its approval of your main demand. If you wish to negotiate for further time, please wave your free arm …'

Lawson remained unmoved, although Bodie, watching through high powered binoculars, saw an almost imperceptable shake of the Colonel's head. 'He's not buying,' he said to Doyle, who smirked and looked away. 'Would you?'

'Why don't they just blow the bloody places up,' said Bodie.

'I was thinking that myself. What would be lost, I wonder, apart from a few jobs …'

Bodie lowered the glasses. 'Government would scream, though. Can't see them agreeing.'

'They might have to,' said Doyle. 'They wouldn't let him explode that thing. Would they?'

He met Bodie's gaze, and each of them frowned. 'I dunno,' said Bodie. 'Maybe not.'

They went back to Cowley, who had just finished speaking into his R/T. 'How's he looking?' asked the Chief.

'Still strong,' said Bodie. 'But the hand is beginning to shake. You can see it is.'

A gas-suited army officer came cumbersomely across to where Cowley was leaning against his own car. 'Hello George,' came the muffled voice from within, and then, hesitantly, took the head-piece off. He was a young major, red faced, his shock of fair hair quite damp with sweat, now.

'Hello John. Any ideas?'

The major said, 'We thought that if anything *did* go wrong we could cover a good deal of the canister. We might be able to contain more than half. Depends on how much of the canister was destroyed in the blast . . .'

Cowley wasn't going along with that. 'It'll scatter the liquid for yards, man. And even if it only tore the canister, how fast could you get there?'

'Not very,' the major conceded. 'But it might reduce the area of affect. If people were evacuated from some two or three square miles, it might –'

'No good,' cut in Cowley. 'I've been in touch with the Chief of Police on that point, and any sort of mass evacuation would lead to uncontrollable jams, not to mention panic. There isn't enough time, and people aren't prepared enough for such quick evacuation . . .'

'My God,' said the major. 'There's no time for anything.'

Cowley glanced at his watch. Bodie noticed that there was a thin sheen of sweat on the man's face, the first time he had ever seen tension beginning to get the better of his Chief. 'Aye,' said Cowley. 'You're right there. There's no time for anything.'

'They'll have to blow,' said Ray Doyle. 'They'll have to destroy their precious research stations.'

'I only wish they would,' agreed George Cowley. 'But the decision isn't ours to make. Maybe you'd like to speak to the P.M., eh? Hurry her along a bit.'

'She knows the full situation?' asked Bodie.

'Of course. But you know her attitude to any sort of blackmail, or terrorism. And besides, Lawson's profile would suggest that if he succeeds with the three target zones already designated . . .'

'He'll go on to three more,' finished Doyle, understanding.

'Precisely.'

'But he can't,' said Bodie. 'His arm isn't that strong.'

Cowley looked at his man with an impassive, almost frightening agreement. 'Aye, lad.'

'Then Lawson is quite likely to be set on dying, and taking half of London with him. Is that what you're saying?'

Cowley affirmed. Bodie and Doyle looked at each other, then sprinted back to the edge of the playground.

'He's thought of everything – those mirrors, no way we could sneak up behind ...' Doyle's dry observations initiated no response from Bodie.

Doyle scanned Lawson from top to bottom, side to side. He searched the edges of the playground, looking for closest approaches, hidden passages, behind equipment, or sheds, but Lawson had picked his spot brilliantly. There was no way of getting close without him seeing.

'Seventy yards from that slide, the most accessible point, behind him. Wearing protective gear we'd never make it ...'

As Doyle talked on, Bodie suddenly froze, dropped the binoculars, glanced round at the anti-gas truck, then back at the motionless figure of Lawson. His eyes began to burn with the glimmering of an idea.

Doyle was saying, 'Even without that gear, and running flat out, you'd be hard pushed ... And it would probably be suicide ... and it might trigger him off too early ...'

'His arm!' yelled Bodie, cutting his colleague off in mid ramble.

Doyle frowned. 'His arm?'

'His arm! It's a blind spot! We could do it!'

They hesitated for just a second, as Doyle looked at Lawson trying to see what Bodie was driving at. They they turned and ran across to Cowley.

'I think I've got it. It's our only chance.'

'Then out with it, man,' said Cowley, the first glimmer of excitement creeping back into his face, as hope rose in his heart.

To Doyle, Bodie said, 'How far from that anti-gas truck to Lawson?'

Doyle glanced at the cumbersome machine that was parked, rear doors facing the playground. It was heavy and slow, because it was designed to muffle explosions in its capacious storage area, and to contain gas and radiation.

'We could get it to seventy yards away without upsetting him. We could get that close ...'

'Right,' enthused Bodie. 'We reverse the truck, flat out, towards him.'

'Never reach him in time,' said Doyle, disappointed. 'He'd see it, pull the chain, and bingo four seconds later. It wouldn't work.'

'The van doesn't *have* to reach him,' pressed Bodie, and looked between the puzzled Doyle and Cowley. 'It only has to go half way!'

'I don't get it,' said Doyle.

'Because I run at him from behind –'

'He'd see you in the mirrors,' said Doyle sharply, and then saw what Bodie had in mind. 'No he wouldn't! Not if you approached him –'

'In the blind spot behind his arm!'

Cowley gasped as he saw the simplicity of the plan, the obviousness of it. 'Can you do it, Bodie?'

Doyle said, 'You start running and at the same time we rev up the gas truck, doors open, full of sandbags. We move slowly towards the arena ...'

Bodie said, 'I run flat out ... have to strip down ...'

Cowley added his own piece of the plan, 'We have marksmen trained on Lawson, waiting ...'

Doyle: 'As soon as he sees you, and he'll see you eventually as you approach ...'

'When I'm on top of him, or when he pulls that pin out ...'

'I drive that truck back at full belt, someone hanging at the back doors, ready to catch ...'

Bodie was flushed, charged up with excitement as the plan could be seen to be workable. 'As he drops the canister, or as he gets hit, I grab it, running flat out ...'

'Four seconds,' said Ray Doyle. 'Just four seconds ...'

'To make the rest of the distance, say thirty or forty yards to the truck, toss it in ...'

'Slam the doors,' said Doyle.

'Bang,' said Cowley quietly. He thought hard for a moment. Then: 'We have no other alternative. Four seconds, with a flying start. Are you fit, Bodie?'

'Fit enough,' said Bodie solemnly.

'Then do it,' said Cowley. 'The man is tiring. There are only minutes left.'

CI5 erupted into action.

Ray Doyle ran swiftly across to the gas truck, took one look at the controls and decided that he ought to leave the driving to an expert. As the man took his position, and got it clear that he was to reverse at maximum speed, in a straight line, Ray Doyle climbed into the bomb-proof space behind the driver's compartment, and set up his position, ready to catch the gasbomb if and when Bodie flung it.

Two sharp-shooters crawled through the bushes and lay flat, Lawson's heart squarely in their sights. They remained in constant touch with Cowley, whose job it was to order them to fire.

And Bodie himself took a track suit and running shoes, brought in by police, and trotted - out of sight of Lawson - round to the rear approach, concealed by undergrowth. Peering through the bushes he could see Lawson from behind, and he didn't need binoculars to tell that the man's whole body was shaking with the effort of maintaining his awkward position.

Quickly, Bodie stripped down to his skin, then hauled on the loose fitting tracksuit. He tied up the running shoes and flexed his feet in them, finding them comfortable and supportive.

He inhaled several times then relaxed, feeling his head clear and his body sharpen up.

Cowley's voice whispered at him from the R/T. 'Ready, 3.7?'

'Just a moment,' he called back, and again peered out at the stationary figure. He gauged again where the blind spot in Lawson's mirror vision would be, and shifted several yards to the left.

He could see, distantly, the flashing lights, and bobbing faces of men, waiting for his signal to commence.

Bodie picked up the transmitter and called Doyle. 'Ready

when you are,' came Doyle's voice. 'No foul passes, now.'

Bodie drew a knife from the small pile of equipment given to him and checked the blade, hefted it in his hand. Through the R/T he could hear the sound of the gas-truck's engine.

Cowley's voice said, '3.7. We're all ready, and standing at starter's orders. In your own time, lad.'

Bodie took four deep breaths to oxygenate, feeling his heart start to race, his vision become acute.

This was it. When he started his run, there was no going back.

One chance, and one chance only. And to fail meant his certain death.

He had to get it right.

For a second his legs trembled, but then he rose to his feet, slapped his knees twice, and raised the R/T to his face, saying, 'I'm coming on three . . .'

He threw the instrument aside, straightened as he counted: One . . .

He took three steps back;

Two . . .

He began to run . . .

THREE!

And he burst out from behind the bushes, running like a hound across the concrete, his spike-less running shoes slapping almost too audibly on the ground.

He had eyes for nothing but the canister above Lawson's still motionless shape. Any second now Lawson would hear him. His legs worked like machines, stretching, straining, pounding him across the distance . . .

Only a few yards . . .

Two shots rang out, and at the same time he became aware of the gas-truck racing into view ahead of him, beyond Lawson.

Lawson's body had crumpled. For a moment after the shots it had remained upright, but now it sank to its knees, the arm still raised, the canister still held high . . .

The pin of the grenade dangled feet above the weapon itself.

Four seconds! Bodie knew he had four seconds. Without effort he began to count: One thousand, two thousand . . .'

He streaked past the body of Lawson, snatching the canister from the hand –

Three thousand

And flung it with all his might at the gaping compartment of the truck, which still was racing towards him. Doyle was screaming something at him, but the words were wind in his ears, meaningless. All he remembered was throwing the canister, yelling with the sharp pain of a twist in his shoulder, then veering to avoid being run over by the truck.

Doyle swung the open doors to, and the sound of an explosion split the air, made the truck itself leap from the ground.

Bodie had fallen to his stomach, and twisted over now as Ray Doyle ran up to him and helped him to his feet. An army of gnome-like men had converged on the truck and were covering it with foam. Cars screeched into the concrete area, and Bodie's ears rang with the sound of running feet, converging on Lawson.

'Bloody good work, mate,' said Ray Doyle. 'Christ you really moved!'

Bodie's lungs heaved and he gasped for breath, managing nothing more than a smile, and a nod. He couldn't get words out because of the thundering of his heart, the gulping of breath.

Cowley came up to him and looked down at him as he stooped, hands on knees.

'Lawson was hit in the heart. Only the way he'd stood for so long enabled him to keep in position for a second after he was dead. That second saved the day.'

There was no response from Bodie, save that he looked up, nodded again. Ray Doyle, still holding his mate by the arm, glanced at Cowley. 'Good run, though.'

Cowley smiled thinly as he watched Bodie's distress. 'You're getting soft, 3.7.' He winked at Doyle.

Bodie straightened up, and nodded agreement. 'Need a long holiday sir.'

Cowley scowled. 'Well, let's not go too far.'

Chapter Eight

Vandals had smashed many of the lights in the underground car park and the place, which was always an eerie and uninviting cavern below the tenement block, now became a terrifying, shadowy void of darkness. Those lights that remained seemed to pick out the shapes of creatures shaped like stone, towering, shambling shapes that haunted the pitch darkness between the rows of parked cars.

Susan Grant always liked to park near to the lift, or to the car park entrance, but tonight she was so late home that she had little choice.

She guided her red Lotus carefully down the ramp from the road to the parking area, scanning the rows of cars, their rear lights seeming to flash as her own headlights picked them out. The parking area was full to the brim.

At last, at the opposite end of the cavern to the lift, she found a narrow vacant lot, and span the wheel of the Lotus to park with a sudden squeal of brakes. She had to squirm out of the door, which wouldn't open fully against the dark Cortina next to her. For a moment or two she left the rear lights of her own car on, while she checked her handbag for her key, and glanced apprehensively about the shadowy, gloomy space that she would have to walk through.

At last she reached into the dashboard and switched off all the lights. She grasped her handbag tightly and began to half walk, half run to where she knew the lift was sited. A single, dim yellow light in the distance was her target . . .

But behind her . . .

She became convinced that the echo of her footfall was no echo. When she stopped, the sound of careful pursuit continued, a heavier footfall, that faltered as someone realised she had stopped to listen.

'Oh Christ, no, not again . . .'

She walked on swiftly, her high heeled shoes clattering on the oil and tyre-marked concrete. The footsteps behind her started up again, and again continued for a few paces after she had stopped, swung round defiantly, and tried to glimpse some shape in the darkness.

'Hey!' she shouted challengingly, trying to keep the tremble out of her voice. 'Whoever you are! Don't you get tired of this?'

There was no response of course. There never was. For the last fortnight, while she had been haunted by this invisible pursuer, there had never been a response . . . And she had never even seen the flicker of a shape, or of movement.

But she wasn't imagining it! She was sane, bright and not scared easily.

Someone was following her; someone was watching her. Day and night, hour by hour. But who, and why?

What did they want with her?

She suddenly turned and raced for the lift, stabbing her finger on the call button and groaning aloud as she heard it move above her somewhere; usually the lift was on the basement floor, waiting.

As she heard the lift approach, she also heard another sound, a chilling, amplified voice, almost hissing out her name:

'Suuuuuusan . . . Suuuuuuusaaaaaaan . . .'

It seemed to be singing her name, calling to her, almost hypnotic. Her face drained of blood, and she flung herself against the lift doors, eyes wide with terror, expecting that at any moment someone would leap at her from the gloom. The lift doors opened and she almost fell into the brilliantly lit interior.

She pressed for her floor and closed her eyes, feeling the tension drain from her body, sensing her shaking legs grow still again. Her wildly beating heart began to slow, and she allowed herself a quick little smile.

When the lift door opened she started to step outside.

A masked man stood there, grey eyes staring at her from the holes slit in the black head-covering he wore. He took a step forward, arm outstretched.

Susan practically collapsed with fright, covering her face with her hands and screaming loudly. A moment later she choked off her own panic, straightened up, feeling bloody-minded enough to kick. Though she shook with terror, her skin clammy and cold, she looked out of the lift again, and when she saw nothing she stepped forward and peered nervously round the corner.

The corridor was empty. Nothing to be seen.

The night porter had heard her scream and he appeared at the emergency stairs, puzzled and plump, holding a night stick. Susan assured him that she was all right, and stepped quickly to her apartment. She fumbled with the key a moment, and finally got the door open.

She opened the door wide before stepping inside, turned on the light, and cautiously entered. The door to the lounge area was open, as she had left it, as was the door to the small bedroom. Quickly she checked round the flat, windows as well, and when she was convinced there was no one here, she returned to the front door, closed and locked it.

Still shaking, still slightly breathless, she walked to the phone and dialled three nines. When the emergency operator answered she said, simply, 'Get me the police . . .'

While she waited for the police to arrive, Susan Grant poured herself a very large gin and tonic, which she drank in two gulps before topping up her glass. Then she changed into slacks and sweater, and brushed through her long hair, trying to compose herself.

She was a tall, attractive girl in her mid-twenties, slimly built but highly athletic. In all probability she could get the better of any attacker, but the weeks of haunting had reduced her certainty on the point. She was so nervous, now, that she would proably give way to fear, if attacked, instead of finding her full reserves of strength.

When Sergeant John Watson turned up she was more composed, and on her third double gin. Watson was a stocky CID man, receding, florid-faced, but cool and very confident as he walked about the well furnished apartment, looking at objects, furniture, and checking the views and vantage points from each of the windows.

'You say the man wore a mask,' he asked her, after she had briefly sketched out the nature of tonight's attack.

'A black ski mask, yes,' she said, and shivered at the memory of those hard, grey eyes watching her so mercilessly.

'And it's happened before ...' Watson flicked back the curtains again and leaned on the window sill, staring across the nightscape of London.

'For the past couple of weeks,' Susan said carefully, 'If I've been late getting back I've heard footsteps.'

'Just footsteps? You've never seen anyone?'

'Not until tonight. Tonight they called my name. It was horrible, mocking. And then the man outside the lift.'

Watson came round the settee and stood looking down at Susan, his hands in the pockets of his suit, his overcoat slung back at the hips. 'Have you reported this before?'

Susan shook her head, sipped her drink.

'Why not?' persisted Watson.

'How do you report just hearing footsteps?'

Watson nodded thoughtfully. 'You must have been frightened. People following you ...'

There was something sceptical in the detective's tone and Susan's hackles rose. 'Contrary to what you may be thinking, Sergeant, I don't frighten that easily.'

Sergeant Watson smiled reassuringly, glancing at the drink in Susan's hand and perhaps wishing he could dare take a drop himself. 'I'm not thinking anything, Miss Grant.'

'Yes you are,' she said, a note of belligerence in her voice. 'You're thinking I'm some kind of attention-seeking hysteric, making it up.'

She rose and crossed to the small trolley where she kept her drinks, placed the glass down with a bang. Watson followed her across the room, saying, 'These late nights – are you often out late?'

Susan tossed back her fair hair, nibbled at her lip for a moment, watching the policeman through green eyes that were suddenly sparkling with resentment. 'No more than anyone else,' she said.

'And tonight ... Where were you tonight?'

'I had dinner with a friend.'

'A man friend?'

Susan shook her head. 'A woman friend, a colleague of mine.'

'But you do have men friends . . .'

Susan drew a deep breath, folded her arms and stared hard at the sergeant. She knew this line of questioning was important, but she still resented the intrusion of privacy. And she didn't like Watson's insensitive casualness, the off-hand way he addressed her as his round face remained implacable, searching. She agreed that she had men friends. She wondered whether to state bluntly that she always slept with them as well.

Watson asked, 'Any particular man friend at the moment?'

'No. Not at the moment.'

'Well,' said Watson, taking his hands from his pockets and starting to button up his coat. 'I'll make a report of course, but . . .'

As he walked to the door Susan cut in sarcastically, 'But since I wasn't mugged, raped or murdered there's not much you can do about it, right?'

'I'll make some inquiries, but without some corroboration there's not a great deal to go on.' He pointed at the drinks tray. 'I'd have a triple, if I were you, and get a good night's sleep.'

'I'll do that,' said Susan sullenly, and went with the man to the door. 'Goodnight. Thank you for coming by.'

When John Watson made out his brief report on Susan Grant's complaint, he was quite confident that this would be the end of the affair. He was surprised, then, and rather shaken to find himself called into the Superintendent's office the next day.

He arrived promptly. The super was seated behind his desk, writing swiftly on a notepad. A second man was in the room, a rugged man in his fifties, greying, steely eyed, dressed in the long, dark great-coat that marked him out as being from the Home Office.

The man was reading his report on Susan Grant. He looked up as Watson entered, and dismissed the policeman after four seconds of penetrating gaze.

Superintendent Patterson said merely, 'This is George Cowley of CI5. John Watson.' And the two men made the merest of acknowledgement of each other.

Watson was then grilled on the subject of Susan Grant. It was a painful few minutes, and Watson rapidly became aware that he'd missed something vital. But he was never to know what. Finally Patterson asked, 'So you thought she was "crying wolf", Sergeant. Did she strike you as the nervous type?'

Watson shrugged. 'Not particularly, sir. But there have been no other reports in that area – none of the other residents have seen anything, nor any of the staff.'

'That's all, sergeant. Thank you.'

Watson acknowledged his dismissal, glanced briefly at Cowley, and left the office.

When he had gone, Cowley snarled, closed the folder. 'The man's a fool. He's not a good man. His report has missed too much.'

Presumably because there was no point in arguing, the Superintendent shrugged off Cowley's criticism, and said merely, 'Well, Major Cowley, I must say that your interest intrigues me . . .'

George Cowley walked thoughtfully across to the desk. 'I know what you're thinking . . . She comes from a family with money, and influence . . . I happen to think she's *not* crying wolf.'

Patterson waited for more, but there was none forthcoming from the quiet, stern-faced Scot. He said, 'You chaps play your cards so close to your chest even a blow torch wouldn't prise them off.'

'Of course,' said Cowley with the hint of a smile. 'That's the nature of the game. May I keep the file?'

'If you sign for it, of course. Good day, Major. Good hunting.'

Ray Doyle was in an extremely good mood, cheered up by the fact of the first sunny day of the year, and by memories of the girl he'd spent the previous night with, and would be seeing again in just about five hours, when he went off duty.

Dressed in a natty dark suit, the collar of his shirt open down to his ribs, he was all ready for the quick addition of a bow-tie to make himself presentable for the club rendezvous that he had with his new-found love.

Bodie was dressed more for action, in faded denims, sneakers and his thin, grey windcheater. He was behind the wheel of the Capri, narrowed eyes intently focused on the red Lotus some yards ahead. His solemn face kept breaking into a boyish grin as Ray Doyle's exuberance carried across to him.

Doyle was asking him silly questions, trying to fill in the boredom of this low intensity pursuit. As a car cut in between him and the Lotus he accelerated, narrowly missed a double decker bus, and slotted into position, one car behind their target.

Doyle said, 'Okay. Try this one. Nine doubleyou.'

Bodie looked quizzical. 'Nine doubleyou?'

'Yeah. That's the *answer* - you think of the question.'

Bodie smirked. 'Oh, yeah, right. Nine doubleyou ... Nope, haven't got a clue. Amaze me.'

Doyle put on an exaggerated Austrian accent. 'Excuse me Herr Wagner, do you spell your name with a V?'

'Oh God,' said Bodie with a grimace, and Doyle grinned broadly as he scored another point.

It was clear to them both that Susan Grant was driving to her office. They had been watching her apartment since the early hours, and so far had seen no sign of anyone suspicious lurking about. Their assignment, now, was to make contact, to try and get Susan Grant into one, or both, of their confidences.

The traffic was heavy, and Bodie demonstrated again his expertise behind the wheel by cutting in front of the forward car, and thus sitting right on Susan Grant's tail.

'Flash car,' observed Doyle, admiringly.

Bodie was looking at the girl's long hair as she drove. 'Flash looking girl,' he said.

'There's the office,' said Doyle, indicating the high building, with its vast expanse of glass windows, that was Susan's work place. 'She'll be looking for a parking spot.'

'Gotcha,' said Bodie with a grin. 'One Bodie special contact manoeuvre coming up.'

They'd gone beyond Susan's office before a parking space presented itself. Susan Grant slowed just beyond the gap, indicating left, and her intention to occupy the space. Bodie slowed the Capri and Susan clearly thought he was allowing her the chance to manoeuvre, but as she reversed into the gap so Bodie swung his own car into the space.

The inevitable contact of front and rear bumper and light was sickening to Bodie, who loved his car; but he knew that the damage was minor compared to some the Capri had sustained. Doyle lurched heavily in his seat, then grinned as he sat back to watch Bodie at work.

The girl jumped out of her Lotus, furious, looked at her shattered light, then straightened as Bodie climbed from his car and walked up to her. She was red-faced and angry, but she was very beautiful and Bodie experienced a strong pang of desire for her as he smiled and shrugged.

Susan said, loudly, 'You could see I was backing in ... You slowed to let me!'

'Sorry,' said Bodie with all the charm he could muster. He looked at the damage, kicked his own front tyre.

'I made all the signals!' said Susan, an edge of hysteria in her voice; she wasn't sure whether to shout or cry. She ran her hand through her fair hair, shaking her head and looking at the calm, dark figure of Bodie.

'It was my fault,' Bodie said. 'I wasn't thinking.'

This puzzled Susan. 'You're *admitting* it?'

Bodie smiled at her, thrust his hands into his pockets and fixed her with his intense, sexy gaze. 'What else can I do?'

Susan was taken aback. She expected to argue in situations like this, and instead found herself melting before the reassuring, pleasant young man. 'Oh ... '

'Listen, I can fix the light. Good as new.'

For the first time Susan smiled a little. She glanced at Ray Doyle, who still sat patiently in the Capri, and Doyle waved at her. Her gaze came back to Bodie, who repeated, 'I can fix it ... if you want.'

'I don't mind,' said Susan, 'I suppose. We ought to exchange insurers, though. Didn't we?'

Bodie ran his fingers lightly over the shattered light, the slight dent in the bumper. 'I'll give you my phone number, if you like. I mean it, seriously: I'll fix the damage. It'll save a lot of hassle. And again, I'm really sorry for the prang.'

Susan relaxed and smiled at last. 'That's all right. And thank you. Yes, fix the light.'

'And you can have the parking space too . . . '

They both laughed, and glanced guiltily, then, at the traffic crawling past them where they blocked the road.

Susan got back into her car, and Bodie did the same, backing up and allowing her to manoeuvre properly into the space. He tucked his own car tightly up against an already parked car, freeing the road more for the passing traffic. Susan locked her Lotus, seemed about to approach Bodie, but shook her head, waved, and went into the building where she worked. Doyle leaned past Bodie and peered at the sign above the door. 'Associated Charities,' he read. 'Never heard of them.' He sat back and looked at Bodie, who was looking smug. 'That's one way to make friends, I suppose.'

'I'm an expert,' quipped Bodie. 'Do it all the time.'

'She's pretty self-assured for a neurotic, wouldn't you say?' But Bodie grinned superiorly. 'My charm overwhelmed her.'

Susan trotted into the offices, but took a moment to glance out of the window at her own car. The Capri that had hit her was nowhere to be seen. For a second she felt a jolt of annoyance that she'd been conned, and would have to pay for the damage herself. Then she smiled to herself, and shrugged. Perhaps it had been worth it. She'd noted the licence plate of the Capri. She ought to be able to track down its driver . . . If the mood ever took her.

She quickly went to the wash room and combed through her hair. Then she entered her own offices, and walked to her desk. Where she worked was a large, open plan arrangement, with small, glass panelled cubicles, and a sense of privacy supplied only by bookshelves. Telephones shrilled and typewriters clattered, and the whole place had a frenetic feel of activity about it.

Her friend Joan Campbell waved a cheery good morning at her as she passed her desk. Susan wanted to speak to Joan, and hesitated, but Joan was tied up with a donor who seemed to want to talk rather than arrange for the transfer of cash. 'Yes sir, your donation can be in any form you wish . . .' she covered the receiver and whispered to Susan, 'A big one. Gotta keep him happy.' And back in the phone. 'We prefer a cheque, sir . . . Yes you can come in yourself . . . My name? Joan Campbell sir . . . ' and so on.

Susan grinned and went to her own desk. Immediately she got there her own phone rang. Without thinking she picked it up, announced herself, and then froze as that same, frightening silence welled up at her. She placed the phone down slowly, almost apprehensively. That moment of good mood had passed in an instant.

She sat down behind the desk, shaking slightly, and started to open the mail that was waiting for her, mostly requests for information about the Charity concerns they represented, and the occasional cheque.

As she dealt with her mail she grew aware that Henry Laughlin was watching her from his own cubby hole. She straightened, uncomfortable to think that the older man should be fixing her with such a lacivious stare, but that was Henry. He'd been making passes at her for weeks, and her patience was wearing thin. Henry waved. Susan smiled briefly, and went back to the task of opening letters.

She had begun to get a headache, a tension headache, something she had been suffering from for days, now, since the silent phone-calls and the following footsteps had begun.

As she was rooting in her bag she suddenly heard her name called, a chilling, mocking sound, the first vowel drawn out, the whole tone that of a song. Her heart raced, and she looked up, but saw Henry Laughlin standing by the coffee dispenser. 'It's me,' he said. 'You were miles away.'

She relaxed immediately and tried her best to smile. 'Sorry, Henry. I was thinking.'

'Coffee?'

'Mm. Yes please, black.'

Laughlin brought the coffee over in its plastic cup. He was in his early fifties, an attractive man, but unmarried. He dressed neatly, and carried himself well, but had the annoying habit of staring at women as if they were bedtime accoutrements. He worked specifically for *Freedom Inc.*, the most popular of the charities under the guardianship of Associated Charities.

'You all right?' he asked, as he sat on Susan's desk and sipped his own plastic cup of coffee. 'You look a bit strained. A bit tired.'

'That's a terrible thing to tell a woman.'

Laughlin looked embarrassed. 'I didn't mean . . . '

'I know what you meant, Henry. I'm all right, truly . . . '

Laughlin's phone rang, back in his cubicle. 'Oh hell. Just when I was building up to another inadvertent insult . . .' He grinned and Susan shared his humour. Laughlin rose and returned to his room.

As Susan bent her head back to work, Laughlin placed his coffee down, sat in his chair and swung his legs onto his desk. He watched Susan Grant all the while as he snatched the phone from its cradle. He said nothing for a minute, just listened, then swivelled round so that his voice would not be audible outside. 'I've told you before. These things take time . . . '

Chapter Nine

Susan Grant worked late that evening, partly because of the backlog of correspondence she had accumulated over the last fortnight, and partly because she hated to leave the security of the premises, where there were always a few members of staff at work until the midnight hour.

But at six o'clock she packed up her briefcase, said goodnight to those hardy souls still working – including Henry Laughlin – and walked swiftly out of the building.

As she passed through the swing-doors at the entrance she was aware that Laughlin, too, had quit work, and was following her out. He'd probably ask her for a drink, and he was always so persistent!

She trotted across the road to her car and had got the key in the lock before she noticed the red rose held in place against the windscreen by the wiper. Smiling, but puzzled, she removed the flower, stared at it, then looked about, wondering who could have made such a gesture. Henry? She glanced over her shoulder and saw Laughling hovering on the steps outside the building, watching her.

Not Henry. He could never think to do anything so delicate as give flowers.

Abruptly, the attractive young man who had broken her rear light was standing beside her. She started with surprise as he appeared, but immediately she relaxed, and smiled.

'By way of an apology,' said Bodie. 'I fixed the light too.'

Susan was overwhelmed, walked to the rear of her car and inspected the damage.

There was no damage to be seen. 'Well I'll be . . . I thought you'd skipped off. I thought I'd been conned.'

Bodie, dressed smartly in a tailored suit with a silk shirt beneath, spread his palms wide as he said, 'You gotta believe.'

'What can I say? The man who tries to pinch my parking space turns out to be a real gentleman.' She glanced up at Laughlin, who was frozen in place on the steps, watching the encounter with Bodie. He seemed grim-faced and angry, and after a moment he started to walk up the street, away from Susan.

Bodie said, 'How about saying you'll have a drink with me?'

Susan raised the rose to smell it, and looked at Bodie across the petals. 'I think I'd like that very much indeed.'

Leaving Susan's Lotus where it was, they drove to a hotel where the bar was quiet, select, and available to the public. After a drink, Bodie suggested food, and Susan, being famished, agreed readily.

They found a quiet corner in Susan's favourite restaurant, *L'Escargot* in Greek Street, and after a substantial meal, and two bottles of a very fine French wine, their hands had touched across the table, and the relationship, though still slightly formal, had at least communicated mutually the fact that there would be no resistance to further development later.

Susan said, 'This has turned out to be a long "drink", and you've hardly told me a thing about yourself.'

Bodie smiled, sipped his wine, and again cast a professional glance around the restaurant, surveying the faces, looking for anyone who was just a little too interested in them. The restaurant communicated only safety.

He said, 'I told you, I like good company, good food, hot sun and cold beer.'

'And what about this "I work for the government"? What does that involve?'

She stared at Bodie across her glass, her wide eyes shining in the candlelight. Bodie lifted up her hand from the table and kissed the fingers, drawing her closer to him. She liked it. He liked it more.

'Just that,' he said. 'I'm a civil servant.'

'So are traffic wardens, refuse collectors . . . '

Bodie smiled. What should he say, he wondered, and how far should he go? 'I'm in security.'

Susan sat back in her chair, eyes widened slightly, the hint of a smile of cynicism on her lips. 'I see. And now what? I suppose I'm expected to say, "How glamorous, you're a spy!" And you're supposed to answer: "No, it's very boring. All paper work".'

Bodie grinned and drained his glass, turning and signalling to the waiter. To Susan he said, 'It's very boring. All paper work. Happy now?'

Bodie paid the bill, fetched Susan's coat, and they stepped out into the cool night air, shivering slightly as they began to walk up towards Soho Square, where the Capri was parked. Susan linked arms with Bodie, and eventually he put his arm round her shoulder. 'I really enjoyed that,' Susan said, 'The meal.'

'That was the general idea. We must do it again.'

'Oh yes, please,' said Susan.

Bodie asked her, 'Do you go out a lot? Or are you a home-bird?'

'I'm not a home-bird, no way. But I don't go out a great deal . . . ' she trailed off, and her step slowed. She was staring ahead, into the shadowy square where rows of cars were parked. Bodie's Capri was just visible, and there was someone sitting on the roof . . .

'There's someone on your car,' she said quietly.

Bodie said, 'I know. Keep walking. I saw him when we left the restaurant. Keep walking, but get ready to do what I say.'

As they approached the car, the youth who was sitting on the roof slid down to the road, straightened, and came towards Bodie. Bodie could see, now, that the boy was dressed in leather, had a punk hairstyle, thick-soled, iron-tipped bother boots, and was holding his right hand in a way that meant, without doubt, that he had a knife concealed in the palm.

Bodie slipped the keys of the Capri to Susan, whispered. 'Get in the car and lock it.'

Then he leapt towards the punk who turned, in sudden panic, and ran down a side street, weaving through the cars, and finally out into a small, open space, shielded from view of the roads by the high, rear walls of several buildings.

Here the youth stopped, turned, and grinned.

The only light was that spilling from a distant lamp, and a window, high up on one of the walls.

Bodie stopped, tensing up, sensing a trap. Sure enough from the darkness around him appeared four other leather jacketed thugs, all young, all very mean looking indeed.

They carried knives, all save one who was swinging a bicycle chain.

Bodie stood very still, watching them close in on him from all sides. He was simultaneously aware of all of them, listening to their breathing, monitoring any hesitation, sussing out the weaknesses in the gang. It was an ability that he'd developed to a fine art during his years as a mercenary. It was part of the art of survival, and he was a master at it.

He had already noticed that the youth with the bicycle chain was over-eager, while the one to his right was nervous. When the punk with the chain made his move, Bodie turned on him, ducked below the swinging metal, and kicked hard and vicious at the boy's chest. He felt ribs give, and heard the bloody moan of the kid brought down.

He swung about, caught the nervous kid in the throat with a swift karate chop, then dodged around the others, sending one of them crashing to the ground with a high kick to the nose, the others recoiling from two immensely powerful punches to their stomachs.

Winded, in pain, startled at the ease with which their target had routed them, they ran into the darkness, all but the first youth who had been broken. He still lay on the ground, face down. Bodie checked his pulse, satisfied himself that the kid was still alive, then returned to the car.

Susan was sitting inside, shaking and almost sobbing.

'What's the matter? You get attacked?' Genuinely concerned, Bodie put his arm around the girl, and she let her head rest against his chest. 'It was the man in the mask again,' she said, her voice tremulous with fear. 'I started to walk after you, and suddenly he was there, running at me. He called my name, that same horrible voice, mocking . . . I ran to the car and he vanished.'

Bodie spent a moment or two more comforting her, staring out into the darkness of the Square. Then he started up the Capri and drove back to Susan's apartment.

He walked into the building with her. She was quiet, unnerved by the double incident of the night. She hadn't even asked how Bodie himself was, being too concerned with the figure that kept following her.

Only in the lift up to her floor did she smile. 'Did you hurt yourself?' she asked. 'I saw you flexing your hand . . . '

'I enjoyed the pain,' said Bodie. 'You OK?'

'Yes. Yes, I'm okay, really. I enjoyed myself tonight, I really did.'

Susan led the way to her apartment, opened the door, and then turned to face Bodie. 'I'd ask you in . . . But it's been a long day. I'm suddenly very tired.'

'Sure,' said Bodie, slightly glumly, but with a resigned smile. He wasn't going to push it tonight. 'I'll call you. Very soon.'

She reached up and kissed him on the lips, just briefly, looking at him for a long moment afterwards, and smiling. 'You do that. I'll be waiting to hear from you.'

'Goodnight Susan.'

''Night, Bodie.'

She closed the door and locked it. Bodie waited outside, listening, as Susan walked about the flat, checking it. When he was sure that there would be no alarm, he turned and left the building.

Susan had indeed checked round the flat, putting on every light in the place, and opening all the cupboards with her heart pounding, and her head dizzy. Everything was all right with one exception.

The bedroom window was open, and hanging loose. Susan was sure she had closed the window before going out. She closed it now, peered outside into the night, then again checked the flat. When she was relaxed again she poured herself a gin, and sat down on her bed, slowly, rather lethargically taking off her blouse and skirt, as she sipped the drink and thought of Bodie.

The phone went and she nearly jumped out of her skin. Picking it up she said nervously, 'Hello? Hello? Who's there?'

After a few seconds of silence, she heard the click of a receiver being replaced.

She hung up, drank down her gin, her hand shaking. The phone went again and she screamed with frustration, picking it up and throwing it onto the bed, standing by the window and staring at the receiver.

She was close to tears. She had no idea what to do. Oh God, why had she let Bodie go? He should have stayed the night. It would have been so much wiser …

Then she heard the voice on the phone, the unmistakable voice of her mother, and almost with relief she flung herself onto the bed, snatched up the receiver and put it to her ear.

'Is that you, Mummy?'

'Yes dear,' came the woman's voice. 'Are you all right?'

'Fine,' said Susan, not wanting to concern her mother with the details of her worry. 'I, er, I dropped the receiver. Sorry. How are you?'

'You sound strange, dear … ' her mother insisted.

'Do I?' Susan shifted round in the bed so she could lie flat, head on the pillow. 'I'm just tired, Mummy, that's all. I need a good night's sleep.'

'I've been calling you all evening.'

'Have you? I've been out.' Her mother was fishing for something, she could tell. The hesitancy in her voice, the failure of the woman at the other end of the phone to get straight to the point, as was usual.

Mrs Grant said, 'Are you coming down this week-end?'

'I don't know, Mummy. I know I said I would, but something's turned up.'

'Oh do come, dear. Cook's longing to feed you up - we both think … '

Irritated, Susan said, 'Oh Mummy, don't fuss so. I've just had an enormous dinner with a charming young man – '

'Well that's something!' cut in her mother's voice. 'I hope he's not another of those weird Chelsea-ites you get in … '

'No he's not,' said Susan. 'Far from it. And that's *all* I'm going to say about him!'

'All right, dear. So off to bed with you. Let me know about Saturday.'

'Goodnight, mother … '

Susan hung up, groaned aloud, then flopped back on the bed, arms and legs flung out, eyes closed.

Mrs Grant placed the receiver back in its cradle, stared at it thoughtfully for a moment, then rose and crossed the room to the open, wood fire, and sat close to it, in a deep armchair. She faced George Cowley, who was smoking a thin cigar and nursing a glass of whisky.

Cowley watched her in silence, waiting for her report.

'She's had dinner,' she said, 'with a "charming young man". One of yours, George?'

Cowley puffed on the cigar, and with a note of cynicism in his voice said, 'Doesn't fit any description I would make, but yes, I think it was.'

Mrs Grant approved. 'Good. I *know* something is going on. Even when she was a little girl she would never admit to being frightened. She would bottle it all up inside.'

George Cowley sipped at his whisky and watched the crackling flames on the logs. 'I wonder where she inherited that from?'

'Am I wasting your time, George?' Mrs Grant stared at her friend, but her mind was more on her daughter than anything.

Cowley said, 'I don't think so. However, I'm not complaining. Sitting here with the very best malt whisky in this lovely house, it takes me back.'

'Anthony, God rest him, felt more at home in your company than anyone else, you know.'

Cowley let his gaze rest on the photograph of Anthony Grant that stood on the small table between them. He was a strong looking man, with a confident, assured smile. His death had affected Cowley deeply, even though Cowley lived and worked with death.

'He was a fine man, Margaret.'

'Since he died, you haven't exactly been a regular guest.'

Cowley drained his glass and placed it down. He rose and smiled and crossed to where Margaret Grant sat watching him. Taking her hand in his he raised it to his lips. 'I was only waiting for an invitation.'

Mrs Grant rose, since Cowley was indicating that he would have to leave. 'Take care of Susan, George. She's very precious to me.'

Cowley shrugged on his coat and walked from the room with her. 'I'll be back in touch before you know it. Good-night Margaret.'

Surveillance: the part of CI5's work that could drive even the strongest willed agent to despair in a matter of hours.

Sitting, watching, waiting, trying to stay awake. Men of

action, men who had fought in the Congo, in South America, in Central Europe, such men could be driven mad by the static process of sitting in a car and waiting for nothing more exciting than to follow another car to its destination, and report on that destination, and then wait some more.

Bodie hated surveillance. But as he sat in the Capri, now, watching the Associated Charities building, he didn't mind one bit that he had sat here for hours, and would stay sat here until Susan Grant left the building.

He'd become personally involved, and was looking forward to the merest glimpse of the girl again.

Ray Doyle climbed into the seat beside him with a cheery, 'Here you go.' He passed a sandwich across. Bodie opened it, and groaned, looking irritably at his colleague.

'It's liver sausage. I can't stand liver sausage. I *hate* liver sausage.'

'So do I,' said Doyle, chewing into a cheese sandwich.

'Then why did you get it?'

'Well, it was just lying there, all on its own, no one interested,' Doyle swallowed his own mouthful. 'I thought, some nice old pig got wasted just to provide that meat. It mustn't be allowed to die in vain . . . ' He grinned as he saw Bodie's expression of true irritation. 'Besides,' he added. 'I forgot that you didn't like it. Sorry.'

Bodie tried to eat the sandwich, but gave up in disgust, placing it on the dashboard, and looking back up at the window where he knew Susan Grant worked.

Doyle peered past him. 'Anyone tried to push her through the window, yet?' His voice had an edge of disbelief, of mockery in it, and Bodie was rankled.

'You don't believe her, do you?'

'Rich kid, fills in her long day collecting for charity. Time drags. They're the type to try and get attention.'

Bodie dismissed Doyle's cynicism. 'The way she looks she doesn't have to *try* and get attention.'

Doyle pigged down the rest of his sandwich, staring ahead through the windscreen and thinking. 'Why d'you think Sir's involved? I mean, what are *we* doing here?'

'You were there,' scowled Bodie, feeling increasingly annoyed with his colleague. 'You heard him. Pick her up, stick with her. Let me know if anything or anyone's bothering her. That's what he said. That's what we're doing.'

Doyle was still rankled at the thought that they weren't totally in the picture. Sullenly he said, 'Nannies Anonymous, that's us . . . '

'It could be worse,' said Bodie. 'She could be fifteen stone with a moustache. What did you suss out about Associated Charities?'

Doyle looked around, bored to distraction by this uneventful assignment, at least as far as he was concerned. 'It's kosher enough,' he said. 'They collect for famine relief, orphans, down-and-outs, old people's homes. You name it. The only cuckoo in the nest is an outfit called Freedom Inc.'

Bodie glanced back at the office, eyes narrowing slightly against the brightness. 'Sounds like a stationer's. What's cuckoo about it?'

'Well they aren't a charity, for one. They campaign to get political prisoners out of jail.'

'Didn't know we put them in,' said Bodie, indifferently.

'Abroad.'

'Ah. You've restored my faith in democracy.'

Doyle went on, 'It's run by a bloke called Henry Laughlin.' He hesitated for a moment, peering past Bodie into the increasingly dense streams of traffic. Then he sat back, picked up Bodie's half-eaten sandwich from where it lay, hot and going stale on the dashboard. 'You're not eating your liver sausage.'

Bodie gave his partner a withering look. 'How'd you like to be force fed?'

Ray Doyle grinned, shook his head, and stepped out of the car. When Bodie was in this sort of contemplative, sour mood, even a joke might cause trouble, and Doyle wanted nothing but sweetness and co-operation for the next few hours.

'Can't sit here chatting all day . . . ' he said, and vanished.

Bodie scowled. He picked up the liver sausage sandwich, gave it the look of a killer about to strike, and wincing horribly managed to choke it down.

Doyle didn't reappear, as Bodie had half expected that he

might. The day dragged on, the CI5 man getting stiff and uncomfortable as he sat, and watched, and waited. He would have given quite a lot to have been able to jog around the block a couple of times, but he knew, from bitter experience in the past, that the moment he was not at his post was the moment his target would leave the building.

At five o'clock precisely, the slim figure of Susan Grant appeared, walking briskly through the revolving doors of the building. She trotted down the steps, blonde hair bouncing about her shoulders, and went straight to her car.

Bodie started up the Capri, fixed his seat belt in place, and watched as Susan's Lotus edged out into the traffic.

He had hardly begun to swing out from the kerb himself, still watching as the Lotus slipped ahead of him, when a grey Ford Escort stopped just by him, blocking his access to the road.

Bodie swore with frustration, glancing ahead to where the red car was still visible, but rapidly disappearing into the distance. He leaned on his horn, then punched it three times, but was rewarded with the view of the driver of the Ford obviously trying to restart the engine. The man was dark, and of middle age, and he looked irritated, as much with his stalled car as with Bodie's impatience.

But he stepped out of the Escort and shouted an apology to Bodie. Shaking his head with irritation, Bodie swung his own car into reverse, and pulled out and round the stationary vehicle.

By the time he was in the traffic stream again, he had lost sight of the Lotus. He thumped the wheel in anger, then did a U-turn in the main road and pulled into the kerb, facing back the way he had come.

He could see the grey Ford just slipping away down a side street. He picked up his R/T.

'Three seven to base . . . I want a trace on a grey Ford Escort, registration number Foxtrot Charlie Mother 486 Mother.'

Angrily, then, he switched off the radio, and drove back to base.

Susan arrived back at her flat quite late evening, after a long shopping spree in the late night supermarket. She had stocked up with provisions, enough food and household supplies for a good two weeks.

She hadn't got *everything* she'd wanted because she'd suddenly become very uncomfortable in the store. There had been a man shopping there, a dark haired, rather pig-faced man, who had seemed to be following her about, staring at her. She had noticed him and he had seen that she'd seen, and had continued to gawp at her in a most offensive and unpleasant way. So she was quite sure that this was just another Henry Laughlin and not the man who had been following her at night.

Although she could never be sure ...

In any event, she had decided that enough was enough and left the supermarket suddenly. She had seen the man follow her out, but he had gone in a different direction and she was sure he had not followed her home.

She went into the kitchen and began to unpack the goods from the large box she had acquired, shelving tins and boxes neatly. Taking out a packet of cereal she was annoyed to notice that the top was open.

'Damn!' she said, thinking that she would have to take it back. Kids, probably, mucking about.

Something about the box disturbed her. She was pretty sure that the box had been perfect when she'd picked it up on the shelf.

Hesitantly, she tore open the top completely, glanced inside, and with a grunt of disgust emptied the contents into the sink.

Among the stream of blood-spattered cornflakes was an immense, rubber spider, whose legs quivered as it lay upside down on the stainless steel, its split belly still oozing the red liquid with which it had been filled.

Chapter Ten

Henry Laughlin lived in a tiny, two roomed flat, whose state of chaos might either be the mark of an intellectual, or of a recluse. The floors and small tables were piled with magazines and papers. The walls were decorated not with paint, but with posters, photographs, and newspaper clippings, for the most part on the subject of human rights. Indeed, on a part of the wall reserved for 'work in progress' a half-finished poster for Freedom Inc. overlooked the room, its tortured, screaming face a terrifying reflection of the mind of the man who was designing it.

Laughlin himself was slumped in a battered, fraying armchair, a pot of tea on the table before him, and the remains of an Indian take-away on the floor beside him. He was distractedly reading an occult novel, which he had bought for its title – *Necromancer* – alone. The word filled him with sinister memories of his own haunted past.

Restlessly, he placed the book down and rose and went to the small fridge where, from among its sparse contents, he drew out a yoghurt. This he took to the window, and spooned it into his mouth as he stared at the street below, and across the several hundred yards to the block of flats where Susan Grant lived.

He was standing there watching when Bodie's Capri drew up and parked on the double yellow lines outside her apartment block. Laughlin's mouth went dry as he watched the youthful man get out of the car and bound up the steps to the front doors.

Turning back into the room, Laughlin flung the half eaten yoghurt across the small living space, watching the sticky contents explode across the half finished poster.

Bodie dangled the hideous rubber spider by one leg, looking at it with an expression of utter horror and loathing. He turned from the sink and dropped the toy into the waste disposal unit, grabbing a paper towel and wiping the filthy, red blood-substitute from his fingers.

'I can't stand spiders,' he said. 'A very sick joke indeed. Who d'you think it is?'

Susan Grant, attractively dressed in a flimsy summer frock, hugged her arms about her body, and stared at the waste unit. She shivered slightly. 'I've no idea.'

Bodie's face was a mask of resentment, a harsh, deadly expression that made him totally unapproachable, lips turned sullenly down, eyes narrowed. 'Ex-boyfriend?' he asked. 'Someone you dumped, someone who can't take no for an answer . . . '

Susan shook her head, moving out of the kitchen and into the lounge. 'No one like that.'

'How about the supermarket? The swap must have been made there. Somebody got close to you. Recognise anyone?'

'There *was* a man in the supermarket staring at me. But it was a . . . dirty look. I know that look very well. And I don't recall him ever getting very close.'

'Probably just a do-it-yourself expert, getting some images for his night games . . . '

As he spoke, Bodie moved towards the door, holding a finger to his lips. Susan frowned, then got the message, and sat down heavily on the arm of the settee. Bodie reached the door, still talking quietly, and placed his hands on the yale lock. Suddenly he yanked the door open.

A man stood there, hand raised to knock at the door. Bodie grabbed him by the shoulder and hurled him into the room.

'Evening all,' he said, and the man cowered.

But Susan had recognised him immediately. 'Henry!'

Henry Laughlin stood shaking in the middle of the room, looking at Susan, and glancing apprehensively at Bodie, who had leaned arrogantly against the door and folded his arms.

Laughlin said, 'I . . . I just dropped by. I didn't know you had company . . . '

'Have a drink' said Susan, and glanced at Bodie with a look that said, ease off, he's harmless.

'No, no thank you,' stuttered Laughlin, and edged back to the door. He kept looking at Bodie. 'I was just passing. I'll see you tomorrow, at the office.'

'All right, Henry. But if you wanted a drink . . . '

'No, really. I should have phoned. See you tomorrow.'

Bodie opened the door and bowed at the waist as Laughlin stepped past him. 'Goodnight,' said Laughlin, and Bodie responded, 'Sleep tight.'

Closing the door, Bodie leaned against it listening; when he was satisfied that Laughlin had gone away he shrugged, came back into the room. 'He was listening outside.'

Susan frowned, shaking her head. 'He wouldn't. Not Henry. He wouldn't do that.'

'Who is he, anyway?' Bodie sat down, staring at the girl.

'He works at the Charity shop. Henry Laughlin. He lives across the street.'

Bodie tapped a finger to the side of his nose. 'Admirer of yours, is he?'

'He fancies me, certainly. But he's too old – '

'Too old? They're never too old!' Bodie grinned.

'Too old for me, is what I was going to say. I don't mind Henry's attentions. He's very lonely.'

'So am I,' said Bodie, and winked theatrically.

Susan smiled and stood up, pouring two drinks at the table. She was puzzled by something, and asked, 'When I called your number I got some sort of switchboard and left a message. But you still got here very fast. Who was I through to?'

Bodie said, cautiously, 'Answering service.' He didn't want her to know that he'd been outside all the time. He didn't think she would take kindly to knowing that her new boyfriend was a secret service man, specifically employed to get her full confidence.

'They found you pretty fast,' she said, offering the drink. Bodie took the glass and raised it, sipping it.

'I happened to ring in. And I was on my way over anyway . . . just on the off chance that you'd have a free hour or so . . .'

'I've got a free evening,' she said.

Bodie looked sad. 'But I'm on duty. And no way of breaking the shift.' He drained his glass. 'So you'll lock up after me. All right?'

Susan stood with him, and kissed him on the cheek. Bodie

snaked his arms round her waist and didn't let her go for a moment, staring down at her through half-lidded eyes. 'I've got to get through the night on that?'

Susan laughed, and reached her lips up towards his. 'I had a feeling you functioned best on four star.'

Ray Doyle trotted down through the sterile white corridors of his wing of the Home Office and burst into the computer room, announcing himself curtly to the security man, and walking across to the first printer.

He coded in his print key and waited for a second as the machine sorted through its files for the information stored on its newest bank. When it printed the file it chattered like a machine gun and Doyle read the information as it appeared on the emerging sheet.

When it had finished printing he tore off the sheet, acknowledged the on-duty operator and left the room.

He found Bodie grabbing a bite to eat, and together they returned to the car, and Bodie drove to their assignment: the same as the day before, parked close to Susan Grant's offices ... on surveillance.

'What've you got?' asked Bodie when they were parked and relaxed.

'Your friend Laughlin is more than a dirty-minded old man. He did four years in Lubianka, though he didn't make the Butlin's camp in Siberia.'

Bodie digested the information, and merely observed that Laughlin was lucky. 'They might have thrown away the key. He got out when?'

Doyle scanned the print-out. 'Two years after the Hungarian uprising. Christ, that's going back. Apparently he was fresh out of University and determined to set the world to rights. Went to Hungary, formed an early version of Freedom Inc., got frozen in Lubianka, then sent home, where he set up the version as we see it today.'

'Still trying to put the world to rights,' said Bodie. 'wonder how he's getting on. Probably reached Watford.'

Doyle grinned, and continued reading. 'He's dedicated to helping, "politicals" everywhere. Oh, and he doesn't like us, CI5.'

'I'm devastated,' said Bodie sarcastically.

'He's written reams on the evils of the secret organisations and societies, even the secret service. "The cancer in our society, the enemy within ..." '

Bodie sneered at that. 'Sounds like a nutter. But I have to say that he doesn't sound like the nutter who's pursuing Susan. Hey, gotta go!'

Susan Grant had appeared at the top of her office steps. Ray Doyle got out of the car, slammed the door and peered in through the window. 'Try not to lose her this time, chuck.'

He grinned and stepped away from the Capri as Bodie edged out, ready to follow Susan as cautiously as possible.

Instead of going to her car, Susan walked on down the street, towards some nearby shops. Bodie cruised about fifty yards behind her, looking for a place to pull in and follow on foot. He had just swerved into a narrow space on the roadside, when he saw a car pull up next to Susan, and a tall, smartly dressed young man step out and confront her.

Bodie left his own car and walked a little closer to observe the meeting. It was clear that the two were arguing, in fact Susan was flushed and furious, and almost hitting her opponent. Eventually the young man gave up, looked frustrated and irritated, and climbed back into his car.

Bodie had to hide in a shop doorway as Susan came pacing back in the direction of her car. When she had passed, Bodie sprinted to the Capri and radioed in.

Susan spent the evening at home, relaxing, doing some repairs to her favourite pair of jeans, watching TV, and finally washing her hair and bathing.

She had just wrapped her hair in a towel, and was thinking of making some cheese on toast, when the telephone rang. She stood in the bathroom and listened to it for a moment, then walked quickly into the lounge and snatched it up. She had gone cold, her naked body covering with goosepimples. But the voice on the phone was sexy, deep and strong, and she relaxed, sat down in the armchair and half closed her eyes.

'Hello Bodie ... Yes, yes ... I'm fine.'

He asked her about the locks, about the windows, about who she might have seen, and she answered reassuringly to every question. 'You can always come round and check me out personally,' she said, and giggled as he told her that he didn't trust her.

He was on duty, so the call was brief. She was much happier as she rose and made to go back to the bathroom, but the phone went almost immediately again.

Without thinking she picked it up. 'Hello?'

There was a moment's pause, and her body went cold. She wrapped her arm around her breasts to try to keep some warmth in her body, but the temperature dropped more and more as she heard her own voice saying 'Hello?' followed by Bodie's sultry tones saying 'Hi, you all right?'

She listened for a long ten seconds, the whole of her previous conversation with Bodie replayed to her. Then she slammed the receiver down and began to shake, feeling the tears surface and begin to well out of her eyes.

Above the silence of her room she heard the sibilant whisper of the terrifying metallic voice that she haunted her the other evening, calling her name in a mocking, sneering way: 'Suuuuuusan. Suuusaaaan! SUUUUUUU-USAANNNN!'

'Shut up! SHUT UP!' she screamed, holding her hands to her ears and finally collapsing into great, racking sobs.

Bodie found out how the trick had been done.

He arrived at Susan's flat within half an hour of her hysterical call to his private number. He dismantled the telephone and found the tiny recording device, a very common telephone tap implacement, and one which he "treated" instantly below the heel of his boot.

'What about the voice?' stuttered Susan. 'The voice calling my name?'

She dragged her housecoat tighter around her body. Her hair hung lank and wet about her shoulders. Her face, without any trace of make-up, looked pale, her eyes red-rimmed.

'One thing at a time, Sue,' said Bodie.

Susan seemed on the verge of tears and Bodie hugged her. She said, 'I don't think I can take much more of this, Bodie. Who *is* it? And why? Why me, what have I done? Who is it, Bodie, who could be so cruel?'

Bodie hugged her even tighter. 'We'll find out very soon. At least we know for sure that they're entering and leaving your flat. They're determined. And that means they're around, and they'll draw attention to themselves very soon.' She shuddered in his arms. He said, 'You know what you need at a time like this?'

Susan looked up at him, and after a moment shook her head.

Bodie smiled. 'Something to take your mind off things.'

He leant down and pressed his lips to hers. After a moment he felt her relax and her lips parted, her tongue touching his own lips in little exploratory darts. The kiss grew fiercer and her hands pulled him closer. The robe slipped open and Bodie reached in to stroke her suddenly warm body.

At last she broke the kiss, but pushed herself close to him, feeling him with every inch of her skin.

Bodie said, 'Is it working?'

Susan smiled. 'Too early to say ...'

Later, when she was more relaxed, Susan curled up on the floor, her head in Bodie's lap. Bodie stroked her hair, but his feeling of relaxation and contentment had to give way to more practical issues.

At last he asked quietly, 'You have a brother, right? Fair haired guy ...'

Susan was surprised that Bodie should have mentioned this. Puzzled, she turned slightly and said, 'Neville? How do you know about Neville?'

'Checked around,' said Bodie. 'What's his problem?'

Susan was too warm and secure to be suspicious. She shrugged. 'He owes money.'

'A lot?'

'A hell of a lot. To pretty heavy people.'

'And he wants you to help out.' It came clear to Bodie immediately, the cause of the anger he had witnessed.

Susan *was* getting a little suspicious now. 'Yes, that's right. How do you know all this, Bodie?'

Bodie ignored her retort and surmised, 'Help that you're no longer prepared to give.'

'Not any more,' said the girl. 'Look, do we have to talk

about my wretched brother –'

She was cut off in mid-sentence as all the lights in the flat went out, plunging them into pitch blackness.

Susan reacted with instant panic. 'The lights! My God –'

Bodie's hands on her shoulders were firm, reassuring grips. 'Calm down, Sue! OK? Calm down . . .'

'Bodie, what's going on?'

He silenced her with a finger pressed firmly across her lips. Peering into the blackness, he listened very carefully. 'Fuse box in the kitchen?' he whispered, and Susan replied, 'Yes . . . in a cupboard, bottom right.'

Bodie rose from his seated position, and felt his way cautiously into the kitchen. He found a box of matches and struck one, and rapidly located the fuse box below the work-shelf. Pressing one of the switches below the bank of fuses, the lights in the flat came on again. 'Miracle of modern science,' he said to the trembling girl who stood in the kitchen doorway.

As Susan made her way to bed, Bodie checked the corridor outside the apartment, and then looked around inside, just to be sure. He stared at the street outside for a long few minutes, but saw nothing suspicious; although it was early, he *did* notice that the lights in Henry Laughlin's flat were not on.

Susan was below the covers, and as Bodie came into the room she said, 'Coming to bed?'

Bodie shook his head. 'Going to do a little checking, first. Try to get some sleep.'

'You won't leave me . . .'

'I'll be back. Honest.' And he leant down and kissed her.

'I'm frightened, Bodie . . .'

'I know. And I don't blame you. But sleep, now.' He put a finger across his lips, turned out the bedside lamp, and left the room.

Bodie's 'little' checking consisted of a lightening tour of the building, from roof to basement car-park, where he picked up a torch, and by lift and emergency stairs. He found no evidence of unauthorised presence, but avoided the night porter with such ease that he realised even an amateur could have come and gone in the apartment block without much difficulty.

He returned to Susan's flat, checked that she was asleep – she was sleeping fitfully, turning from side to side, and making little noises in her throat – and after deciding not to wake her and give her something to relax her charged-up system, he lay down on the couch. And listened.

About an hour later he was roused from his light doze by a faint scratching sound. He was instantly alert, although his body hardly moved a muscle.

Slowly he raised his torch, then flicked it on, swept it round the room, his left hand holding his magnum ready to challenge any intruder.

The room was deserted, but the scratching sound persisted, like a rat, he thought, a rat or mice in the walls, scrabbling to get in.

He walked to the far wall and the scratching sound grew louder. He moved along the wall, ear pressed to the plaster, until he was sure he was close. A small pile of plaster dust on the skirting board below a picture seemed to tell the story. Carefully he shifted the picture to one side, and saw a tiny hole in the wall.

The scratching sound stopped, then started again. Bodie replaced the picture and crept back to the bedroom, where he shook Susan awake.

'What's the matter?' she whispered, as she got over her initial shock.

'Who lives next door to your lounge?'

'No one,' she said. 'It's empty. They moved out . . .'

Bodie pressed his finger to her lips. 'Stay put,' he said. 'I'll be back in a minute or so.'

He went back to the lounge, keeping the light off, and opened the curtains. Outside was a small balcony, just big enough for one person to sit on; the balcony of the adjacent flat was a short stretch away, and Bodie climbed between them with ease.

He opened the locked window with his knife, a talent he had mastered years ago, and stepped into the dark interior of the deserted flat. A thin shaft of yellow light was visible under one of the doors leading off from the lounge.

Bodie drew his gun and crossed the room on tip-toe, listening at the door for a second before flinging it open. He burst in and dropped to a crouch, the gun held in both hands before him. Quickly he covered every corner of the room with eye and gun-barrel, then breathed a sigh, not of relief but of irritation, as he stood up and relaxed. The room was deserted. The whole apartment was empty.

He went back into the lounge and, by the light from the other room where the naked bulb burned brightly, he could see a long rod sticking out of the wall that separated this flat from Susan's. On the floor below it was a hand-drill, the cause of the scratching noise.

Bodie peered through the hole in the wall, then out of the corner of his eye he saw a small tape recorder on the floor. He picked it up, pressed the play button.

A haunting, mocking voice whispered, 'Suuuuuusan!' Over and over again. Bodie grinned humourlessly. He had suspected *this* particular trick. But obviously he had disturbed whoever had been working here as he was coming across between the balconies. Where had that worker gone, he wondered?

Next door, Susan waited in the lounge in darkness, shivering despite her housecoat and slippers. She watched the open window, and listened, but everything was quiet.

She was startled by a knock at the door of her flat, and padded quietly across to it, leaning against it and listening before asking, through the wood, 'Who is it...?'

'Me. Bodie. Open up,' came the voice back, and with a relieved smile Susan undid the catch.

She opened the door to let Bodie in, but the masked man stood there, grey eyes glittering evilly from behind his black woollen face-piece. Before Susan could scream, or call for help, one of his hands was on her throat, the other slapped across her mouth. He forced her back into the room, then twisted her violently round, still keeping her dumb with his powerful hand, forcing her down, now, onto the couch, her arm twisted agonisingly behind her.

She began to struggle for breath, but her face was pressed into the cushion, and though her body heaved and racked, the air would not come.

As panic rose in her, she started to kick out, and her foot struck the drinks tray, sending it crashing to the floor. The masked man reacted with a muttered oath, the first time Susan had heard any voice from him. Immediately she felt herself dragged from the couch and into the bedroom, still unable to scream, but able to breath again.

Her legs were like jelly, and the man practically carried her through the door, and into a hiding space beside the wardrobe. Here he stood, holding her crushingly still in front of him, her own body shielding his.

The hand that had been threatening to rip her arm from its sockets released its grip, but a moment later she felt the ice cold touch of gun metal on her cheek.

Silence, then; the waiting game.

Bodie would have heard the drinks tray go over. He would come. Wouldn't he? Sure enough, a minute or so later Susan heard the unmistakable sound of a man moving the couch in the lounge, not walking round it cleanly. Susan's heart started to race. The gun metal on her cheek changed angle so that the muzzle was aimed at the bedroom door.

A second later the bedroom light went on, and a blur of shape rolled across the floor, rose into a crouched position, heavy hand-gun pointed squarely at her. Bodie's eyes were wide, his face white with tension and panic. He had *almost* shot, but Susan was screening the enemy too well.

She sensed that the man who held her was about to fire; he jerked slightly, moving the gun to get a better angle on Bodie.

That was the moment when Susan used her free left arm, still hanging limp and painful, to grab the masked man in the most painful place she could think, at the same time ducking forward.

The man yelled. There was a double explosion that deafened her, and something warm trickled on her neck. The grip on her arm relaxed as the man's heavy weight bore down on her back. She wriggled free, found herself in Bodie's arms, and only glanced briefly at the dead man, his black-suited chest a blossoming rose of redness.

After the inevitable invasion of police and curious bystanders, Bodie stayed with Susan while Ray Doyle, who had been first on the scene, went with the corpse to the Home Office Mortuary. He radioed in to Cowley that the dead man had had no identification on him, so he was going along to the morgue to see what the pathologist had to say.

Cowley's gruff tones on the R/T seemed almost tiumphant. 'So much for the Cry Wolf theory.'

Doyle acknowledged that grimly as he rode in the ambulance. 'Yeah ... Wolf, or Wolves ...'

It took about half an hour to set the mortuary up for the sort of examination that Doyle needed to conduct on the dead man. He was called in to the cold, glaringly lit room, by a police doctor. There were only two assistants at the autopsy, and Doyle stood well back from the slab, not liking to see in too much detail what was to be done.

For his own purposes, however, he needed only the superficial details.

The doctor lifted limbs, prodded, turned and scrutinised the clammy, naked body before him. 'Lateral scar on the right upper thigh, a vaccination mark on the right leg –'

Doyle, noting this down, looked up. 'Could he be South or Central American? That's common there ...'

'Could be,' said the doctor, 'But the blood group, skin pigmentation, everything suggests British parentage. Frankly he could be –'

'An Eskimo, right?' Doyle was slightly irritated. He wasn't going to get anywhere, he could see that now. 'Maybe his fingerprints will show ...'

The doctor cut across him. 'That's certainly your best chance. Now, where was I. Vaccination mark on right leg ...'

Doyle continued to take notes, feeling cold and hungry and miserable. He thought of Bodie, snug in that warm apartment with the girl, and resolved that the next time they were sent to make contact with a young, female target, *he'd* do the driving.

The drawing room was elegant, richly decorated with gold-framed paintings, marble statues and many other priceless art objects. A log fire burned brightly and the room was pleasant with the odour of pine smoke.

The man who reclined in a deep armchair, side-on to the fire, was clipping his nails with a solid gold trimmer. He was in his forties, elegantly dressed in smoking jacket and flannels. When he had ceased to play with his nails he drew a fat cigar from his pocket and used the nail-pairers to clip the end of it.

Across the room stood a dark haired man, shabbily dressed, and worried. If Bodie had been in the room at that moment he would have remembered the face from the Escort that had stalled in his path, a couple of days before.

'I don't know what went wrong, Mister Bauer,' stuttered the frightened man.

Bauer smiled cruelly. 'So it would seem, Miller. I ordered you and Smith to perform a simple eradication, a boyfriend, a tough young man but not invincible. Instead of which one of you ends up in a police mortuary.'

Bauer turned cold eyes on the other man.

'He's got Laughlin jumping too, this boyfriend. He's more than he seems. He carries a gun, for a start. Only the police do that here.'

Bauer acknowledged the point with a wave of his cigar. 'You're right, Miller. I was forgetting we weren't in South America now.' He drew thoughtfully on the cigar, blew a thick cloud of blue smoke into the air.

'What do you want us to do, Mister Bauer?' prompted Miller, nervously shuffling forward.

Bauer said, 'Watch every move they make. The girl has a parent in the country and often goes there. Wherever she goes I want to know.' He fixed Miller with a cold stare, appraising the almost useless man, but aware that he had little choice but to utilise Miller's undoubted ability as an assassin, at least this one last time. 'I want the boyfriend dead. I want it done properly. And I want to get the girl too. We should have done it a long time ago.'

He turned away from Miller, who nodded and left the room.

In silence, Bauer contemplated the crackling log fire.

Chapter Eleven

In Bodie's estimation, the apartment was no longer safe. The dead man had certainly been acting under orders, and there would be more where he'd come from. The best way for Susan to lose herself for a few days, Bodie reckoned, was to go out to the country and stay with her mother.

And the best thing for he himself to do, Bodie further reasoned, was to keep an eye on her ... By going to her country house with her.

Before dawn Susan had packed a few things in a small travelling case, and was being hustled down the stairs to the car-park, where Bodie's Capri was located.

But since the police had left she had been slightly sullen, slightly suspicious. As she packed she started to question Bodie, and the questioning went on relentlessly.

Now, as they hurried through the dark, underground park, her voice carried through the stillness with irritable insistence. 'But just to let us go, no questions, no statements. Just like that! You knew one of them, didn't you?'

'What did you want them to do?' asked Bodie sourly. 'Arrest me?'

'And the gun,' Susan persisted. 'They didn't even ask for your gun!'

'It must have slipped their minds,' said Bodie with the hint of a smile.

But Susan had cottoned on, and almost resentfully she said, 'That time you bumped into my car - you did it on purpose.'

'What can I say?' said Bodie, hurrying her faster towards the Capri.

'It's been an assignment, hasn't it? You've been assigned to take care of me ...'

'I could make it a life's work, Sue, quite happily. It's been very worthwhile, taking care of you.'

He unlocked his car, chucked Susan's case into the back,

and let her in to the passenger seat. Susan went on, 'But what do you know about that man? Who was he?'

Bodie said, simply, 'They'll find out. My job is to protect you. Belt up. If you see what I mean . . .'

As Susan fixed the seat belt she said, 'Now I know where I saw that good looking one before . . . Mr Doyle. He was in your car that day . . .'

She was thrown backwards as Bodie revved up the Capri and fairly flew out of the parking space, running noisily up the ramp and out into the early morning streets.

'The curly haired one, yes. He just sat there and grinned. He's your partner. I knew I'd seen him before . . .'

Bodie ignored her. He drove west as fast as he dared.

They reached Susan's country home less than two hours later. It was a grand house, eight bedroomed, and it stood in more than two acres of its own ground, hidden from the surrounding neighbourhood by tall pines and squat, gnarled oaks that looked many hundreds of years old.

It was breakfast time, and Bodie and Susan sat opposite each other at the table, hungrily awaiting eggs and bacon. Susan's mother sat at the head of the table, pouring coffee from a silver pot. She was smiling, and delighted to see her daughter, but kept casting searching looks at Bodie, unsure what to make of the unshaven, dark man whom her daughter found so fascinating.

'I've heard of dropping in for dinner, but breakfast . . . This *is* a nice surprise,' she said.

Susan grinned. 'You're always saying I don't come over enough.'

Mrs Grant looked pleasantly at Bodie. '*And* you don't usually bring your friends.'

Bodie sipped coffee. 'Perhaps she's turned over a new leaf, Mrs Grant.'

Mrs Grant laughed. 'You've brightened my weekend. Now tell me, Mister Bodie, what is it you do?'

Bodie exchanged a quick glance with Susan, who was smirking behind her cup. He said, 'Er, I'm in security.'

Mrs Grant wasn't sure how to take that. Puzzled, she said, 'How interesting. What is it you secure?'

Susan chipped in with, 'You, mother, for one.'

'Me?'

Bodie added, 'I work for the government.'

Mrs Grant seemed a little more impressed now, although she said, 'I can't say the government has ever made me feel secure. When Susan's father died he left a great deal of money. What the government gave me after all the death duties and Lord knows what duties was hardly enough to feed the cat.' She smiled at Bodie, who tried to share the humour. The maid brought in breakfast and Bodie's eyes lit up at the sight of the huge plate of fried sausages, bacon and eggs.

Susan was saying, 'Mother, you're shameless. You're absolutely rolling in it.'

Bodie was half way through a mouthful of food when Mrs Grant asked him, bluntly and abruptly, 'Are you a gold digger, Mister Bodie?'

'Mother!' cried out Susan, shocked and embarrassed by this blatant rudeness. But Bodie just grinned and nodded. When he finished the mouthful of food he said, 'A hundred per cent. When I look at your daughter I see fast cars, big yachts, and the South of France. Then there'd be all that alimony she'd have to pay me when we split up.'

Susan stared at Bodie, eyes wide, mouth gaping, not knowing whether to laugh or hide her face. She glanced at her mother expecting an explosion, but Mrs Grant was chuckling to herself.

'I like him, Susan. He reminds me of your father.'

Susan was relieved, and kicked Bodie beneath the table. 'That's something, at least!'

Later in the morning, Susan gave Bodie a conducted tour round the house and grounds. Bodie was much impressed, and could hardly credit that any single house could have so much room inside. But it was outside that he enjoyed himself most, walking hand in hand with Susan through the trees, by the small lake in the grounds, and along a quiet, overgrown pathway towards the edge of the property.

He had been hoping for seclusion, but a rusty iron gate gave access to the roadway beyond, and through this gate, as they ambled towards it, the tall, lean figure of Susan's brother suddenly appeared.

'Hello Neville,' she said, as Neville strolled up to them. He looked suspiciously at Bodie, before stooping to peck his sister on the cheek. 'Who's this?' he asked rudely.

'My name's Bodie. How'd you do.'

Neville ignored him coldly. 'Mother in the house?' he asked Susan, who nodded. Neville strode off, Susan and Bodie watching.

'You may have made a hit with mother, but not with him.'

'I'm shattered,' said Bodie. 'But impressed by his old world charm. Besides,' he took Susan in his arms, 'It's the mother I have to win to win the girl, not the brother.'

'Oh yes?' said Susan, as if to say 'what are you up to?' 'And are you trying to win the girl?'

'We'll see,' said Bodie, and they continued walking.

But Bodie was intrigued by Neville, and he guided them around the grounds, until eventually they came back to the house by the side path. There was something about Neville that Bodie didn't trust, but he wasn't sure whether or not to tell Susan so.

He decided to keep quiet, but as they approached the house it was clear that Neville was much less interested in discretion. His voice, raised in anger, could be heard coming from the study.

'Why? Why won't you? A few thousand – it's petty cash to you!'

Mrs Grant's voice was soft, firm and clear. 'I've told you, Neville. I'm sick and tired of telling you why.'

Bodie stopped by the open window and looked at Susan, who made a grim face and shook her head. 'He's always trying to scrounge,' she said.

From the study Neville pleaded that, 'This time it'll be different. I swear it . . .'

'How many times have I heard that.' Mrs Grant's voice became tinged with sadness. 'How many times have I paid your debts, only to see you make the same stupid mistakes all over again . . .'

Neville's voice was rich with resentment. 'Susan's been brainwashing you again.'

'No she has not. You're thirty-one, Neville. You've been bankrupt *twice*. You're at the mercy of every glib-talking con-man who crosses your path. Giving you money is like giving a gun to a baby.'

'All right,' rasped Neville, clearly devastated and furious by the refusal. 'If you won't help your own son, I'll find another way. I hope it doesn't upset your gracious living.'

He stormed out of the room, pushed past Bodie and Susan as they entered through the front door of the house, and strode briskly and sullenly out of the grounds.

The dead man's fingerprints were enough to identify him. Doyle had spent an hour with Cowley looking at videos, and a small home office file of Edward James Smith. He'd only had a single arrest, but had been under occasional surveillance for several years. Ultra right-wing affiliations, mostly in Europe and South America. The file suggested that he was a hit man. It would have been useful to have talked to him, but Bodie had got there first.

One thing was clear, there was an organisation behind the haunting of Susan Grant; and they knew that Bodie was in active service.

After the meeting with Cowley, Ray Doyle forced entry into Henry Laughlin's premises, leaving no mark on the door to suggest he had done so.

He searched around the flat in a vague, distracted way, then bugged the phone as neatly as he could, and checked that the monitoring van could receive him clearly. That done he proceeded to check through drawers, shelves and cupboards, looking for anything that might help CI5 understand Henry Laughlin a little better.

Anything that might indicate *who*, exactly, he was, and whether he might be involved with the group that were terrifying Susan Grant.

He checked most carefully through the contents of Laughlin's desk, replacing every item, every sheaf of paper with great care. It was mostly press-cuttings in a variety of languages, letters, photographs of political prisoners, and scribbled notes. But in one of the drawers, hidden among several sheets of typed paper, he found a photograph of a girl in school uniform. She looked about twelve years old, and the snap-shot was taken in the country somewhere. She looked very like Susan Grant.

Deeper in the same drawer he found several newspaper cuttings that were not related to political prisoners, but to

Susan Grant herself. Mostly cut from the society page, especially from the Daily Mail, they showed Susan over several years at clubs, discos, and society balls.

Laughlin had quite a dossier on the girl.

Doyle closed the drawer and frowned, trying to think through the implications of this. Did Laughlin have a crush on the girl, as she suspected? Perhaps it was as simple as that. But something didn't smell right to Ray Doyle.

He left the flat and went to the monitoring van, and not a moment too soon. As he walked out of the building he saw Henry Laughlin himself strolling down the street, home from work early.

In the van Doyle waited, and after a few minutes the monitoring equipment showed that Laughlin was making a phone call. Doyle placed the headphones on and listened. A woman answered, Laughlin asked for a man called Mason, but Mason wasn't available. Laughlin left the message that he needed to speak to Mister Mason urgently. It was about Bauer, he said. Very urgent.

Bodie spent a very pleasant evening indeed, drinking good scotch, making eyes at Susan, and chatting with Susan and her mother about any number of things. They had looked through photograph albums, and run a couple of home movies, and the concerns and care of CI5 had begun to seem a long way away.

Bodie had learned, during a rather glum few minutes, that Susan was in fact Mrs Grant's adopted daughter. Susan's natural parents had been killed in a plane crash when she was very young. The fact that Neville was her step-brother went a long way to explain the hostility felt between the two of them.

They went to bed about ten o'clock. Bodie's room, the guest room closest to Susan's, was freezing, but Bodie didn't contemplate sleep for some time.

Rather he took a jog around the grounds, in the darkness, and continually checked Susan's room to make sure everything was as it should have been.

It was about midnight that he heard the creak of a floorboard outside his room, and he reacted instantly.

Opening his door a fraction he saw the shadowy shape of

a masked man stepping lightly towards Susan's room. As the man opened the door, Bodie edged down the corridor wall behind him, gun in his hand, and stepped across the hallway, avoiding the ancient floorboards as best he could.

Peering into the room he could see the man approaching Susan's sleeping form, and he caught the first whiff of chloroform.

He hadn't even woken the girl, or got the pad near to her face, before the cold, snub nose of Bodie's magnum had rammed into the back of his head.

'You ought to go back to school, chum,' snarled Bodie. 'You're losing your touch.'

Within an hour the man, who had declared that his name was Joseph Miller, but had said nothing apart from that, was securely ensconced with the County Police headquarters, in a cramped interview room.

George Cowley and Ray Doyle had arrived promptly from London, and they crowded in on the impassive man, who sat nonchalant and unbothered.

He may have been losing his technique at night games, but he was well trained in keeping his cool against the sort of battering that CI5 could dish out. But then, he was from South America. He was trained to resist interrogation; it would have been second nature to him. He wouldn't talk until the blow lamps started to sizzle him, or the electric current reached a thousand volts.

He had said, with a smile of derision on his face, that he had been burglarising the house. After the silver.

Cowley sneered, but recognised that this was just game playing. 'What were you going to do, chloroform it?'

Miller nodded, and smiled. 'That's right.'

Ray Doyle leaned towards the man, one hand on each of the arms of the chair. 'And your friend, the one who got himself killed. Was he after the silver?' Doyle's face, though angry, was too boyish to upset an old pro like this.

Miller just said, 'I don't know anything about anyone getting killed.'

Cowley's soft, accented voice whispered in Miller's ear, 'And I suppose you don't know anything about trying to frighten the young woman to death?'

'Now what young woman would that be? There are so many ...'

So eventually they gave up. Cowley was exasperated, but it was clear that this man was a small pawn in a much bigger game. They'd just have to wait until the bigger fish appeared on the scene.

Miller was taken to the cells, and Doyle and Cowley drove back to London. They were surprised, then, to be called back to the County Headquarters in the middle of the following afternoon.

As they stepped into the station they could feel the tension.

They were taken below.

What appeared to have happened was that, some hours earlier, a man had arrived at the station, announcing himself as Miller's solicitor. Miller had made the call earlier, and since this was pure routine the man was conducted below. The police Constable who had accompanied the solicitor had heard Miller call him by the name Bauer.

Bauer had been in his young middle age, a smart, elegantly dressed man, meticulously manicured, his greying hair perfectly trimmed. He had worn gold rings, had carried a slick, expensive looking brief-case, and had had the sort of superior air about him that the Constable usually associated with young barristers.

He and Miller had talked quietly for a while, and when Bauer had left, Miller had been seated casually on his uncomfortable cell chair, looking out of the high, barred window.

Two hours later, when the Constable had brought him some lunch, Miller had still been sitting there. Reason? A needle wound in the base of his neck, right through to the spinal cord.

Cyanide, the pathologist discovered. A massive dose injected quickly. Neat, said Ray Doyle, shuddering at the thought of that particularly hideous death. Yes, said the pathologist. Neat cyanide.

'We must find this Bauer, and quickly,' said Cowley as they left the station. 'Where's the girl?'

'Back at work,' said Doyle. 'Bodie's on his spot again. I think the surveillance is becoming a labour of love.'

Cowley made a disapproving sound, but said, 'We'll leave him there for the moment. You have a job, now. Get in the car.'

Doyle slipped in the passenger seat of Cowley's dark limousine, and Cowley switched on a small tape-recorder. 'This was recorded a couple of hours back during the surveillance on Henry Laughlin.'

As the spools turned Doyle heard Laughlin's voice saying, 'Hello?'

The caller said, 'Laughlin? It's Mason. I couldn't get back to you yesterday.'

'Never mind that,' snapped Laughlin. 'We've got to move, and fast. It may be too late. I *must* see you.'

That was all, except that Mason agreed to meet Henry Laughlin within fifteen minutes.

'Mason has been identified as a solicitor, working for Mason, Gould and Partners. Here's the address. Make him co-operate.'

Ray Doyle returned to his own car and sped back to London. He parked hurriedly and almost ran up the front steps of the tall building near Gray's Inn Road. Inside the offices of Mason and Gould he found a very strict secretary, young, but highly efficient. 'I'm afraid it's impossible to see Mister Mason without an appointment,' she said, and though Doyle tried a standard, seductive smile, she was having none of it. Doyle looked irritated for a second, then flashed his identity card under the girl's nose.

'I'm sorry, but without –'

Cutting her short, Doyle walked to an office door. 'This his office?' Without waiting for her to reply he barged into the room. 'Mason?'

'Just a moment!' shouted the man who sat behind the desk, working at a file. 'Who the devil?'

'The name's Doyle,' said Doyle, closing the door to the office and going across to the desk. He showed his ID. 'CI5. Tell your secretary to get off the phone to the police.'

Mason had frozen slightly as he saw the ID. He glanced nervously between the card and the impassive, staring face of the young man. Then he reached out, snapped on the intercom, and told Miss Wilkes to relax.

'What do you want with me?'

'Henry Laughlin,' said Doyle bluntly. 'You know him, right?'

'We . . . that is, I act for him in certain matters.'

'We know. You spoke to him on the phone, a couple of hours ago. You met him by arrangement at short notice.'

Mason was incensed. His chubby face reddened brightly. 'Phone tapping! Just a minute, Mister –'

'Doyle. And no, the regulations were not infringed. And it's not your phone that's tapped. We have reason to believe that your client is implicated in a serious crime. A girl's life is threatened. So I want some answers from you, and I want them fast.'

Henry Laughlin was furious. He felt betrayed, betrayed by the one person he had always trusted. Red faced, almost apoplectic, he paced around the room, kicking furniture, slapping his hands against his legs, trying to stop the raging tide of anger that bubbled from him.

'All my political life I've fought against the invisible governments, the faceless wielders of power! And you've set them on me!'

He whirled to face his betrayer, stabbed a finger accusingly at her. 'You of *all* people!'

Mrs Grant stared back, impassive and cool.

'Henry, I've done nothing of the kind. Now calm down, *please*!'

'Calm down? You're forcing my hand at every turn. I should never have taken the chance and come here, but I have no chances left!'

Mrs Grant stepped towards Laughlin and tried to smile. 'Henry, you *must* believe me. George Cowley was a friend of Anthony's, a friend even from before the time we married. When I sensed that Susan was in danger, I asked him to look into it.'

Henry Laughlin was almost in despair. 'But Margaret, he's with CI5 . . . That's worse than MI5. MI5 at least have some moral responsibility. CI5 have a licence to kill, to maim, to destroy. It's evil, and those men are evil. Cowley is a sort of Big Brother. He's answerable only to the very top, and given *carte blanche* apart from that.'

Margaret Grant snapped, 'And now he's protecting Susan. And that's my first concern! It should have been yours . . .'

Laughlin sobered up instantly, stared at Margaret Grant, and slowly nodded his head. 'I know. I know. I know why she's being harrassed, and I've put an end to it.' He sank down into a chair, put his head in his hands and murmured. 'I've put an end to it at last. God help me. God help me . . .'

Wearing dirty denim jeans with matching jacket, and a grubby white tee-shirt next to his skin, Ray Doyle looked every bit the casual gardener that he was pretending to be. He weeded in and out of a flower bed, near to the main entrance of a local common. There were quite a few people about, dog-owners, joggers, a football match taking place somewhere further across the park.

Doyle was quite inconspicuous as he worked, waiting for Mason to turn up and make a rendezvous with the South American agent, Bauer.

He was pretty sure that Bauer was already in the park. His agent's nose sensed it; it kept twitching. He kept feeling the hair on his neck prickle.

As he wheeled his gardener's barrow about this end of the park he took every opportunity to scan the grounds for a sign of the man described by Mason. Twice he had caught the flash of sunlight on a lens, coming from some high, bush-covered ground about three hundred yards away.

He was sure that Bauer was surveying the park with binoculars, and he kept his head down, and the appearance of hard work as authentic as possible.

At last Mason appeared, walking in through the main gates, carrying his attaché case.

Doyle picked up his barrow and wheeled it off to the left, stopping every so often to pick up a piece of litter and cast a quick glance at the solicitor. Eventually he saw a plump, well-dressed man walking towards Mason, swaggering as he strolled with a cane. There were binoculars on his chest.

Using natural cover Doyle got closer, and witnessed Mason pass the attaché case across to Bauer. Bauer opened the case took out the small box of tapes, and some papers, and transferred them to his binocular case. He then turned and began to walk away from Mason, deeper into the park, but towards the farther entrance.

Mason glanced at Doyle, then turned and walked away.

Henry Laughlin's tapes had been passed over. He had kept his part of the bargain, through the mediation of his solicitor, and now it was up to CI5.

Doyle ran quickly after the South American, overtook him under cover of undergrowth, and stepped out onto the pathway ahead of the man, close to where the amateur football match was taking place.

'Mister Bauer?' he called, and expected the man to freeze.

Instead, Bauer panicked, broke into a run, and despite the appearance of middle age fairly fled across the football pitch, legs pumping, body vanishing at a sprint.

Doyle drew his magnum and gave pursuit, but he couldn't fire with so many people around. Bauer used the cover of the players excellently, but tripped over one of them, and dropped the binocular case.

Although he scrambled to his feet and continued to run, he left the case where it was. Doyle, close behind, got struck by the football, and an angry group of youths closed in on him, complaining bitterly that he was disturbing their game.

By the time he had shouted 'Police', flashed his gun, and earned the respectful sight of the youths scattering, Bauer was at the road, and running out of sight beyond traffic.

Damn, thought Doyle. Clutching the binocular case he ran to his own car, and radioed in that he had lost Bauer, but got the tapes. That was bad news for Laughlin, and bad news for Susan. Bodie took the news at his stake-out of Susan's offices. 'Understood,' he said quietly. 'He'll think Laughlin set him up. He's got no choice but to get Susan, now, so stay ready.'

In the park grounds Doyle nodded, agreed, and got into his car.

Chapter Twelve

The offices of Associated Charities functioned normally, and as noisily as ever, and only Joan noticed Susan Grant's distracted manner. When Susan assured her that everything was all right, the other girl shrugged, and walked away, but called back, 'Must be quite a relief not to have Henry staring at you . . .'

'Yes . . .' said Susan, and glanced at Laughlin's empty cubicle. The older man had not been in today, nor had he rang in to say he was sick, or delayed.

Towards the end of the day, Susan spent more and more time at the end window of the floor, peering down at the street where Bodie sat quietly, but attentively in his car. She knew he was attentive because every time she looked down so two of his fingers made an almost imperceptable waving motion. Just once he had glanced up at her and smiled.

That single smile, that single link between the two of them, had made Susan feel very relaxed, very confident.

Bodie had said that she might be the target of a man called Bauer, that he might try to make contact with her, or entice her out of the building. She was nervous about that, but it was impossible to be too nervous with your own personal, highly trained warrior, looking out for you down below.

And once she'd left work, she would spend the evening with Bodie anyway.

It was nearly going home time.

Guiltily, Susan looked at the pile of unanswered correspondence on her desk, and reluctantly she sat down to work at it. Joan packed up, swept by to ask Susan if she would like a quick drink, but Susan declined.

'I've been slow all day, I'd better work a few more minutes.'

When she left the building, and went with Bodie, she didn't want anyone else seeing her. So she decided to let

Joan and the others go first, and follow about five minutes after.

Below, in the street, Bodie watched people leaving the building and caught Susan's glance down from her office, tapping her watch as if to say 'not much longer'. Bodie slipped out of his car and fetched a paper from a street vendor, searching the main road carefully as he did so, but not spotting anyone who came close to the description of Bauer.

He read the paper fleetingly, keeping his eye on the main entrance to Associated Charities. The traffic was heavy, rush hour traffic, and moving quite slowly.

A van blocked his view for a few seconds, then moved on. Bodie thought nothing of that. Vans and buses had fleetingly blocked his view of the entrance way all afternoon.

But he might have noticed that the swing doors were still swinging ...

Someone had gone in ...

Inside Susan's office, a phone rang. Susan was already in her coat, and ready to leave, and had waved goodnight to the last of the secretaries to depart. Business before pleasure, she decided, and picked the phone from its cradle.

It was a standard inquiry, and she leaned down on the desk, propped on her elbows as she answered it.

'Yes, that's right sir, I am ... You wish to make a donation? Certainly. How much were you thinking of giving?'

The man at the other end said, 'Ten thousand pounds.'

Susan was surprised. One rarely received so generous an offer, and there was a special routine involved for all donations in excess of one thousand pounds. 'That's very generous indeed, sir ...'

'Let's say it's a matter of conscience,' said the caller. 'But please, just briefly, would you outline some of the activities of Associated Charities?'

Susan glanced at her watch, and sighed slightly. But there was nothing else for it. 'Certainly sir.'

She started to speak, telling him that their main function was to raise money, food and supplies for the undernourished areas of the world. As she spoke she crossed to the window and let Bodie see that she was engaged. Below, peering up, he shrugged.

'We have people working in every country that we are aiding. They supervise the disbursement of the funds and the distribution of supplies. Do you have any questions? Sir . . . are you still there . . . ?'

The man had gone. For a second Susan was puzzled. Then she heard a motor-horn blast, and she heard it twice . . . Through the window, and through the phone.

Her hair prickled on her neck. Her face frowned. Had the man been ringing from somewhere in the building?

And then she smelled chloroform!

She dropped the phone and whirled round, but too late. The tall man was on her, his arms round her, the sweet smelling, overpowering chemical rammed against her face on an ice-cold pad of cloth.

She screamed, kicked over a chair, and struggled. The pad wasn't quite across her nose and mouth, but she began to feel dizzy, and the man was so strong, bending her down to the floor, his left hand and arm crushing across her chest, stifling her . . .

Her hand closed on a small vase, but it was a heavy china object and, though the man tried desperately to drag her away from the window, she managed to twist round, and fling the vase through the glass. It shattered the window.

Susan prayed that Bodie would notice.

In a final, desperate attempt to avoid being rendered unconscious, she bit at the wrist that held the pad, and felt the skin break. The man yelled, struck her on the face with his hand, but dropped the chloroformed pad. He began to drag her bodily across the office, and when she tried to kick he punched her sickeningly in the stomach, and then chopped her on the back of the neck.

She went limp, weakened by the pain and the stunning shock. He could have done that in the first place, and saved a lot of effort, but it was too late now. He half dragged, half carried her out of the office, to the stairs . . .

Where the athletic shape of Bodie could be seen, powering up to Susan's level.

Immediately the man bent Susan's limp form over the stair-rails. She hung precariously, more over the rails than safe, and she screamed as she saw the long drop swimming before her. 'Hold it, Bauer!' shouted Bodie, and raised his magnum.

'Drop the gun or she goes over!' shouted Bauer, and let Susan slip a little so that she slid further to oblivion, and screeched in panic.

'Drop the gun!'

Bodie did as he was told.

Bauer ordered, 'Now back down the stairs. Slowly. No tricks.'

As Bodie did this, so Bauer edged down the stairway, holding Susan across the rail and sliding her down, one step at a time. When he reached Bodie's gun he picked it up, smiled, and scratched his sweating forehead with the barrel. He yanked Susan off the rail and stood her up, holding the magnum to her temple, and twisting both her arms up behind her back.

'I've got nothing to lose,' Bauer said, and Bodie's eyes narrowed slightly, his gaze flickered between the man and Susan, whose tearful face was held grimly in an expression of desperate control.

Bauer ordered Bodie to fetch his car immediately outside the entrance. 'Any tricks and I'll kill her, and do my damndest to kill you too. Now go fetch . . .'

Bodie fairly sprinted across the road, revved up the Capri and swung it round, outside the building. He quickly switched on the R/T and called Control.

'This is 3.7, I've got trouble. Put me through to Alpha and 4.5. But tell them, for God's sake to keep radio silence.'

As he finished he left the set switched on, but pushed it into the glove compartment and hoped that Bauer wouldn't notice.

Bauer came running down the steps with Susan, glancing both ways, the gun hidden between him and the girl. He pushed Susan past the passenger seat, into the back, and climbed in beside her. Leaning forward, he nudged Bodie's face with his own gun.

'Drive. Exactly as I tell you. Keep looking straight ahead.'

'Where are we going?' asked Bodie.

'Just drive!'

'All right, all right, but give me a clue. I mean do I turn right or left or what?' He sounded petulant and irritated, and he tried to sound a little frightened too.

Bauer just said, 'Drive south, over the bridge.'

'Will do.'

Some miles away, George Cowley listened intently to every bit of information feeding back from Bodie's radio. He could hear Bauer's voice saying, 'Turn right at the roundabout', and he leaned forward, following that on a large scale map of south London. Switching on a different connection, he contacted Ray Doyle, who was trailing Bodie by a few hundred yards.

'Keep going for three miles,' said Bauer, and Bodie repeated the instruction, sounding like a man who was speaking just for the sake of making a noise, to ease the silent boredom.

Bodie was saying, 'What the hell do you want her for, anyway? Why not let her go?'

Bauer rasped, 'Shut up. I told you to drive, now keep quiet.'

'First you try to scare her, then you try to kill her. And now where are you taking her. I don't – '

And abruptly the voice of the CI5 man died, the link was closed.

'Damn,' said George Cowley, and through the R/T with Doyle he heard Ray Doyle swear as well, in frustration, and irritation, and perhaps a little concern.

'Nice try,' said Cowley to an aide, 'But he talked too much.'

The aide was working at a small televisual screen, on which an occasional fuzzy blip was appearing. 'We're getting his Tracker signal ... muddy, but it's coming through.'

'Well that's something at least,' said Cowley. To Doyle, over the radio, he said, 'I'm looking at the map, projecting his route, and there's a possibility coming up: the old airstrip at Padley. Though Bodie's being led a drunkard's walk, that's in their mean direction. It's a possibility.'

'A definite maybe,' called back Doyle.

'Go for it,' said Cowley, watching the Tracker signal on the magnified route grid. 'The Met police are alerting all mobiles, and looking out for the Capri, but Bauer's obviously armed, and would quite happily kill the girl . . .'

'On my way, Control.'

For a split second Bodie had expected to hear the explosion of the magnum, and see blood and skull pasting the back window of the car.

Bauer was furious, and actually struck him on the back of the head, a jolting blow that made the Capri veer as Bodie saw stars, and felt shooting pain.

'Very clever,' said Bauer, holding up the now useless R/T. 'Smart enough to get you killed, that's how clever.'

'Wouldn't be fun if I didn't try a trick or two,' said Bodie, trying to sound cold, trying to let Susan know that he was still more in command than perhaps Bauer realised.

'Turn left here,' said Bauer angrily, 'Then first right.'

Bodie said, 'The full Magical Mystery Tour, eh?'

'To you, perhaps.'

Within minutes of leaving the more densely populated regions of South London, Bodie began to get an inkling of where they were headed. Ten minutes later he knew for sure, catching a distant glimpse of the large expanse of deserted grass and concrete.

The Padley airstrip!

It was a place used, now, mainly for storing cars, prior to their export. The runways were cracked and overgrown, and sheep grazed the grass where once bombers and fighters had skidded and burned on their return from wartime Europe.

Bodie knew the place well. He and Doyle had twice before had encounters in its deserted huts, shelters and hangars.

He smiled grimly as Bauer ordered him off the road, and along the winding approach track, that cut through a now-deserted gate house and onto the fields leading to the runways. The car lurched and bumped across the uneven ground, and Bodie frantically tried to assess whether or not a bit of expeditious driving might throw Bauer off his guard. But Bauer was onto his thoughts, and the South American sat back in the seat, pressed the gun hard against Susan's skull.

'Quickly,' he said, 'Get to that strip. And no tricks.'

Bodie saw, ahead of them, and part hidden behind a row of some twenty Talbot cars, a small light aircraft, a make that he didn't instantly recognise, with markings that didn't ring true.

How the hell he had got that in through London's highly secured airspace, Bodie couldn't imagine. But presumably Bauer was intending to use the same way out.

He braked the car sharply, close to the aircraft, and looked about, wondering whether he might spot the shadowy shape of a policeman, or even Doyle, lurking in one of the ramshackle Nissen huts. But he doubted that Doyle would have got here before him, and Cowley would not have asked the police to come in, not with the girl's life at stake.

'Give me the keys,' snapped Bauer, and Bodie handed them across the seat, conscious of the man's trigger finger squeezed tight on the magnum. Susan looked terrified, deathly white. Perhaps she sensed that Bodie would not, after all, be able to save her from abduction.

They all got out of the car. Bauer flung the keys as far as he could into the grass, and then pointed the gun at Bodie.

'Start walking. With your hands up, that direction. Don't look back. If I see you running, or not doing as I say, I'll happily kill this girl.'

Bodie stared at him for a minute, then gave Susan a smile, tried to communicate by pure thought that there was no way he was going to let Bauer get away with this.

But he couldn't decide whether Bauer was bluffing or not about taking the girl's life. And she was too precious to risk.

He turned and put his hands on his head. He started to walk, very slowly.

Behind him, Bauer prodded Susan Grant with the gun, and hussled her up the steps and into the aircraft. He made her put her hands on her head, and sit in the cramped rear seat.

'I'm watching you in the mirror,' he said. 'And I have very fast reflexes.'

Bauer was in the pilot's seat, fiddling with the controls. Susan could see Bodie still ambling slowly away from them. Bauer's eyes were constantly on her in the wide mirror that he had placed on the aircraft's dashboard.

The engine hummed, then bumped and roared into life, the whole fuselage shaking with the energy of it. Distantly, Susan heard the sound of a car, screeching brakes, revving engine, and she glanced out of the small side window to see a sleek TR7 racing across the field towards the craft.

Bauer saw it too and panicked, making the plane lurch forward in fits and starts. As it did so, the magnum slipped from his lap onto the floor.

Bauer cursed, tried to reach for the gun, but had to keep his hands on the wheel as the plane began to taxi slowly down the runway.

Susan could wait no longer. She smashed out with her balled fist and knocked Bauer forward against the controls, and as he was taken by surprise, and shouting angrily, she tore back the door and leapt from the plane.

Bauer's hand grabbed at her blouse and the fabric ripped as she fell. She hit the concrete painfully on her side, and rolled, but her arm had jarred with pain, and it nagged her. She stayed, half sitting, half crouched on the ground, watching as the TR7 streaked after the plane.

Behind the wheel she could glimpse the curly-haired shape of Ray Doyle, his face set hard, but with a smile on his lips that told of his excitement.

'Get behind a car!' yelled Bodie, who had turned and broken into a run, back towards Susan.

The aircraft turned as well, facing back towards the two of them, and coming at them at full speed, its engines roaring, the grim face of Bauer white and determined in the cockpit.

Bodie reached Susan and dragged her to her feet, racing across the path of the aircraft as it roared past, dropping to the ground as Bauer raised the magnum and fired two shots at them.

The rounds struck the dirt about two feet away. Bodie felt the shockwave.

Doyle had turned his own car, and now streaked past the aircraft, trying to head it off the runway. But Bauer was too expert a pilot to be taken in by such tricks (the car wouldn't sacrifice itself, it was merely trying to panic the pilot) and he kept on straight, trying to get enough ground speed for his take off.

Doyle accelerated ahead of the plane, turned side on and raised his own heavy-duty magnum.

As the craft raced past, Doyle calmly, coldly shot Bauer through the head. The man slumped over the controls, the aircraft zigzagged wildly for a moment, then pitched over onto one wing.

Doyle went back to his car and drove away, watching in his mirror as the plane exploded into fire.

Bodie and Susan stood waiting for him.

'Thank you,' said the girl, shaking visibly. 'Thank you both.'

'All in the line of duty,' said Doyle. 'I didn't mean to kill him,' he said to Bodie. 'My hand shook.'

Bodie's eyes twinkled. 'Of course. I can't be bothered to look for my keys. How about a lift home?'

Doyle grinned. 'Three in a TR7?'

'Cosy,' said Susan.

They stood for a moment, then, and watched the plane consumed by fire, black smoke rising into the afternoon sky like a funeral pyre.

Susan returned to her mother's place, accompanied by Bodie, Doyle and George Cowley. She found Henry Laughlin there, and was surprised. Cowley took her by the arm, and they walked in the garden. Doyle and Mrs Grant took a stroll in the rose gardens. Bodie chatted to Laughlin, filling in a few of the gaps in CI5's record of the previous day's events.

'Mr Laughlin,' said Cowley, 'Is an idealist and a brave man. His commitment to freedom of political thought is absolute.'

Susan smiled. 'Poor old Henry. I never knew he had such secret talents.'

Cowley glanced at her, steeling himself for what he had to tell her. She would have to know that she had misunderstood Henry Laughlin's interest in her totally.

'When he alone was at risk, he was unshakeable.' Cowley waved the small box of tapes. 'He was quite determined to release this evidence of torture used on political prisoners in Central America, but the government of that country sought to prevent him from doing so, and they found a way.

They sent Bauer, an agent, to threaten the safety of the one person he truly cared about in his life.'

Susan frowned. 'Me? Henry cared about me more than anyone else?'

Cowley stopped, turned to face her. 'You'd care about *your* daughter, wouldn't you?'

For a moment Susan was too stunned to speak. The blood had drained from her face. 'What are you saying? That Henry Laughlin is my father?'

Cowley nodded. 'That's right.'

Susan couldn't cope with this. She shook her head. 'My parents were both killed in a crash. I was adopted by the Grants because of that . . . both my parents were killed . . . '

Cowley took her by the arm, started to steer her back round the garden to where Laughlin stood, half chatting to Bodie, half watching his daughter, waiting . . .

'Your mother was killed in the crash, when you were just a little girl. Your father survived the crash, but because of what he was doing, and where he was, he was arrested, and imprisoned for years. During that time your adoption was arranged by close friends of his. When he was released it was felt that your happiness was secure and should not be disturbed. Would you . . . ' he raised the box of tapes, and held them out to Susan as they walked. 'Would you like to return these to him now?'

Susan hesitated a moment, then took the box. She looked up at Cowley, and smiled. 'Funny old Henry . . . My father.'

'A brave man,' Cowley repeated, and Susan nodded agreement.

She walked away from Cowley, and Laughlin strolled to meet her.

Cowley walked across to Mrs Grant, and she stood at his approach, and linked arms with Ray Doyle, who smiled broadly at his chief.

'This young man has been advising me about my roses, George.'

Cowley was surprised. '*This* young man? Really?'

Ray Doyle said, with a smirk, 'Didn't you know I've got green fingers, sir?'

Cowley laughed. They all three watched Susan as she hugged her father.